CARTOON NETWORK

BEN 10

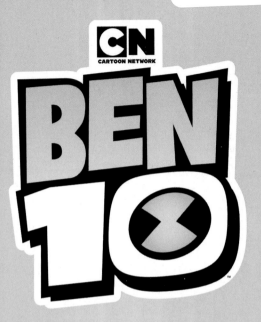

FOR SCIENCE!

kaboom!

BEN 10: FOR SCIENCE!, July 2019. Published by KaBOOM!,
a division of Boom Entertainment, Inc. Ben 10, CARTOON
NETWORK, the logos, and all related characters and elements
are trademarks of and © Cartoon Network. A WarnerMedia
Company. All rights reserved. (S19). KaBOOM!™ and the
KaBOOM! logo are trademarks of Boom Entertainment, Inc.,
registered in various countries and categories. All characters,
events, and institutions depicted herein are fictional. Any
similarity between any of the names, characters, persons,
events, and/or institutions in this publication to actual names,
characters, and persons, whether living or dead, events,
and/or institutions is unintended and purely coincidental.
KaBOOM! does not read or accept unsolicited submissions
of ideas, stories, or artwork.

For information regarding the CPSIA on this printed material,
call: (203) 595-3636 and provide reference #RICH – 847297.

BOOM! Studios, 5670 Wilshire Boulevard, Suite 400,
Los Angeles, CA 90036-5679.

Printed in USA. First Printing.

ISBN: 978-1-68415-373-2
eISBN: 978-1-64144-356-2

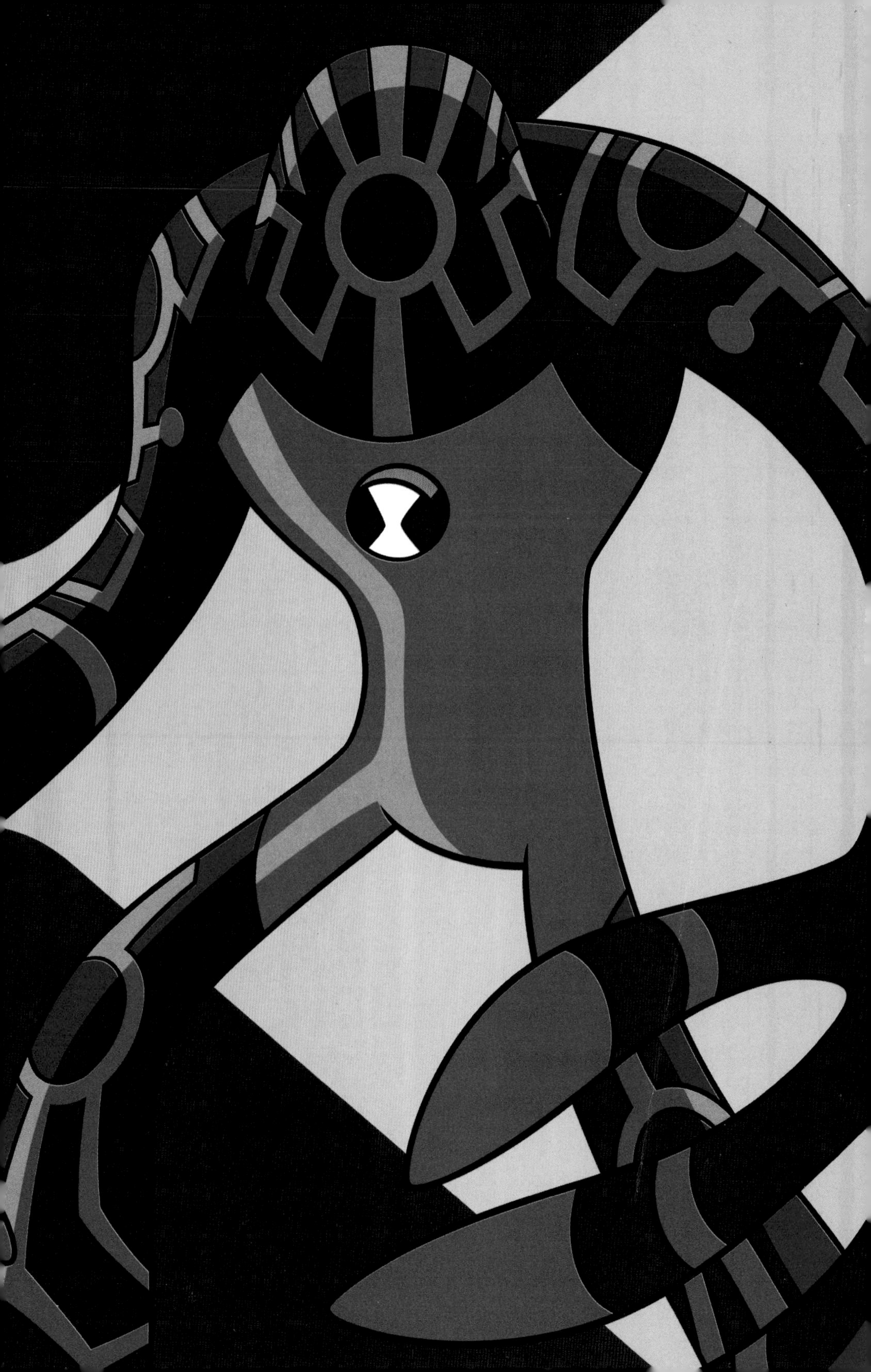

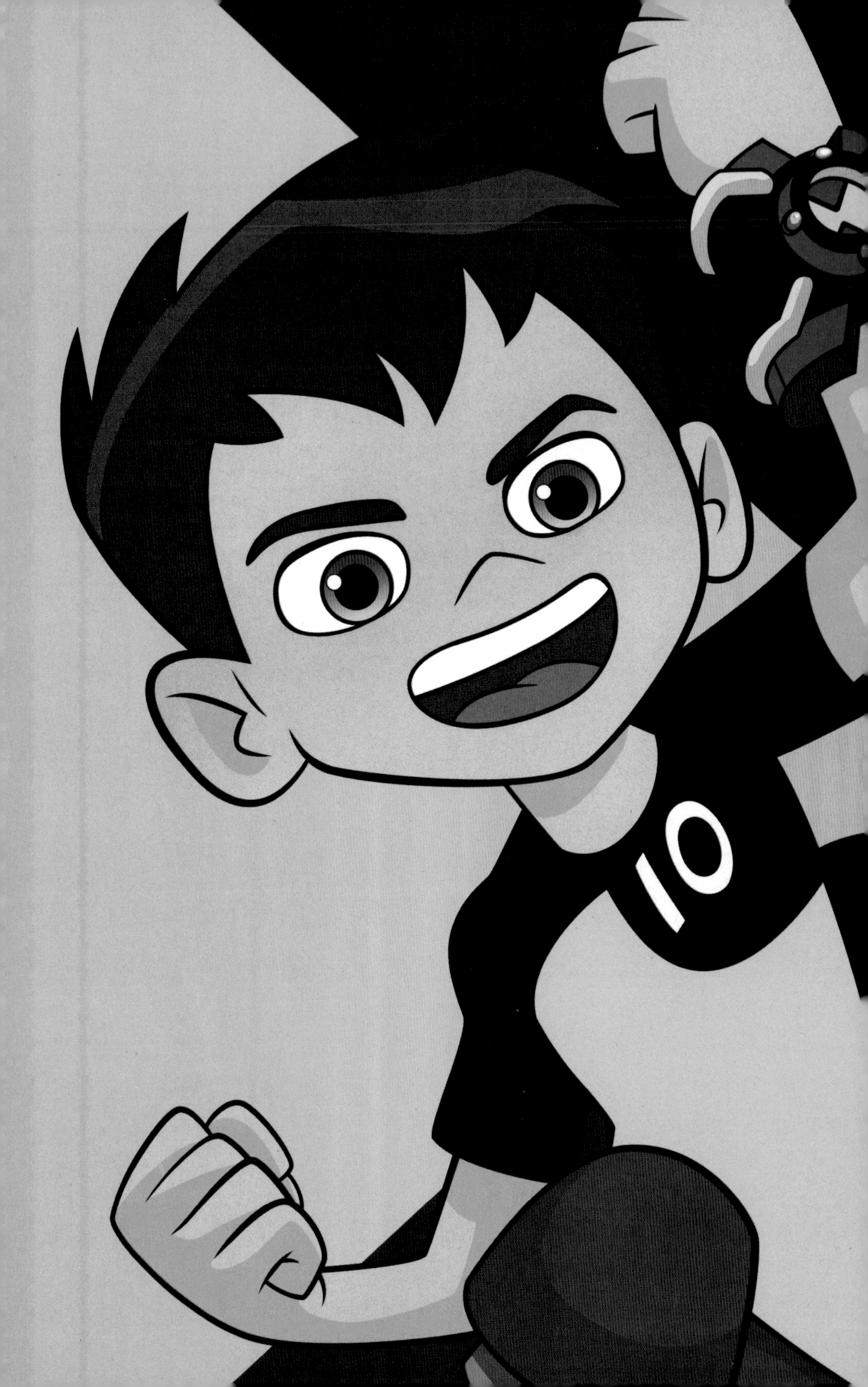
10

BEN TENNYSON IN...
FOR SCIENCE!

CREATED BY
MAN OF ACTION

WRITTEN BY
C.B. LEE

ILLUSTRATED BY
MATTIA DI MEO

COLORED BY
ELEONORA BRUNI

LETTERED BY
WARREN MONTGOMERY

COVER BY
MATTIA DI MEO

DESIGNER
JILLIAN CRAB

ASSISTANT EDITOR
MICHAEL MOCCIO

EDITOR
MATTHEW LEVINE

WITH SPECIAL THANKS TO
**MARISA MARIONAKIS, JANET NO,
AUSTIN PAGE, TRAMM WIGZELL,
KEITH FAY, SHAREENA CARLSON,**
AND THE WONDERFUL FOLKS AT
CARTOON NETWORK.

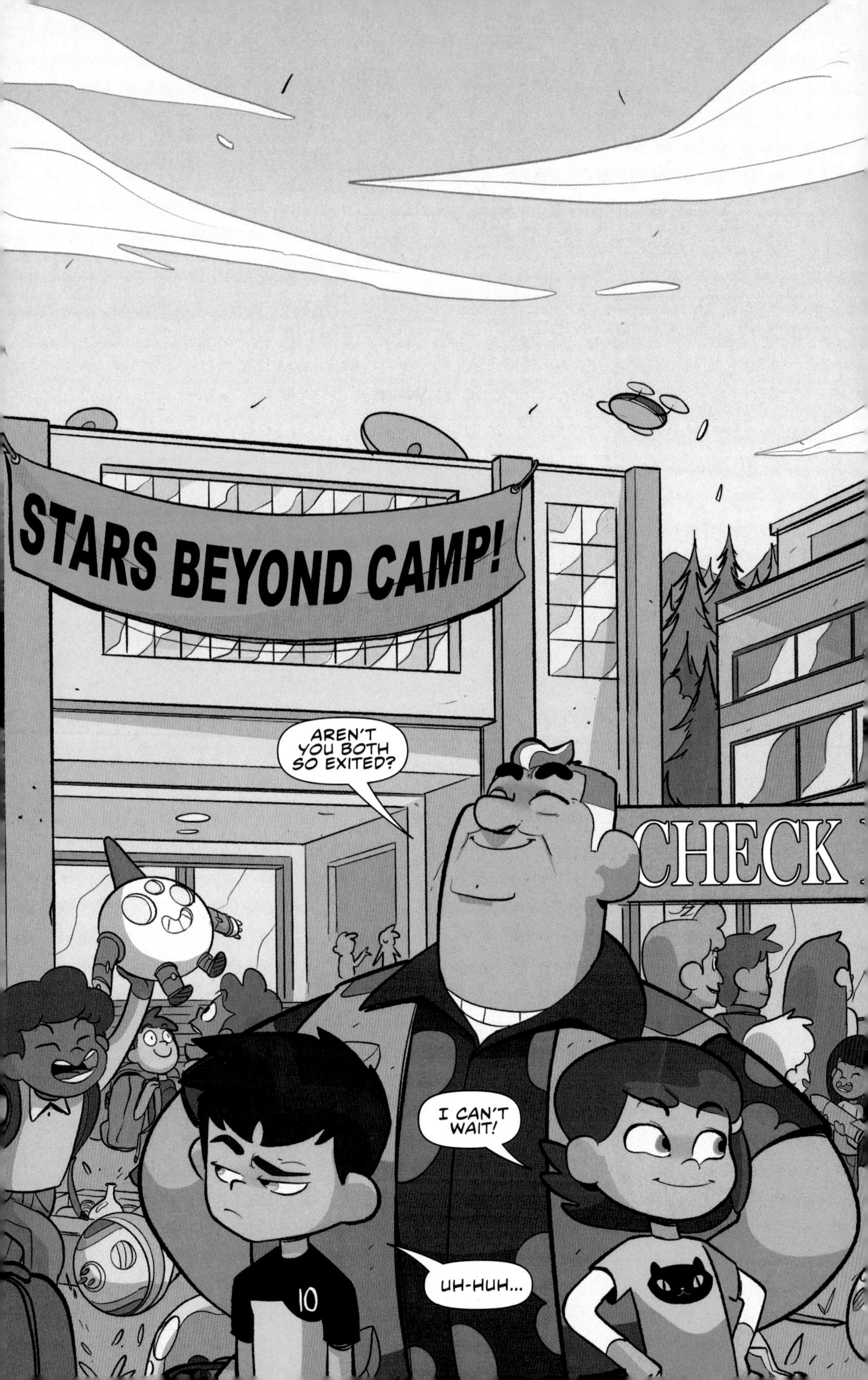
STARS BEYOND CAMP!
CHECK
AREN'T YOU BOTH SO EXITED?
I CAN'T WAIT!
UH-HUH...
10

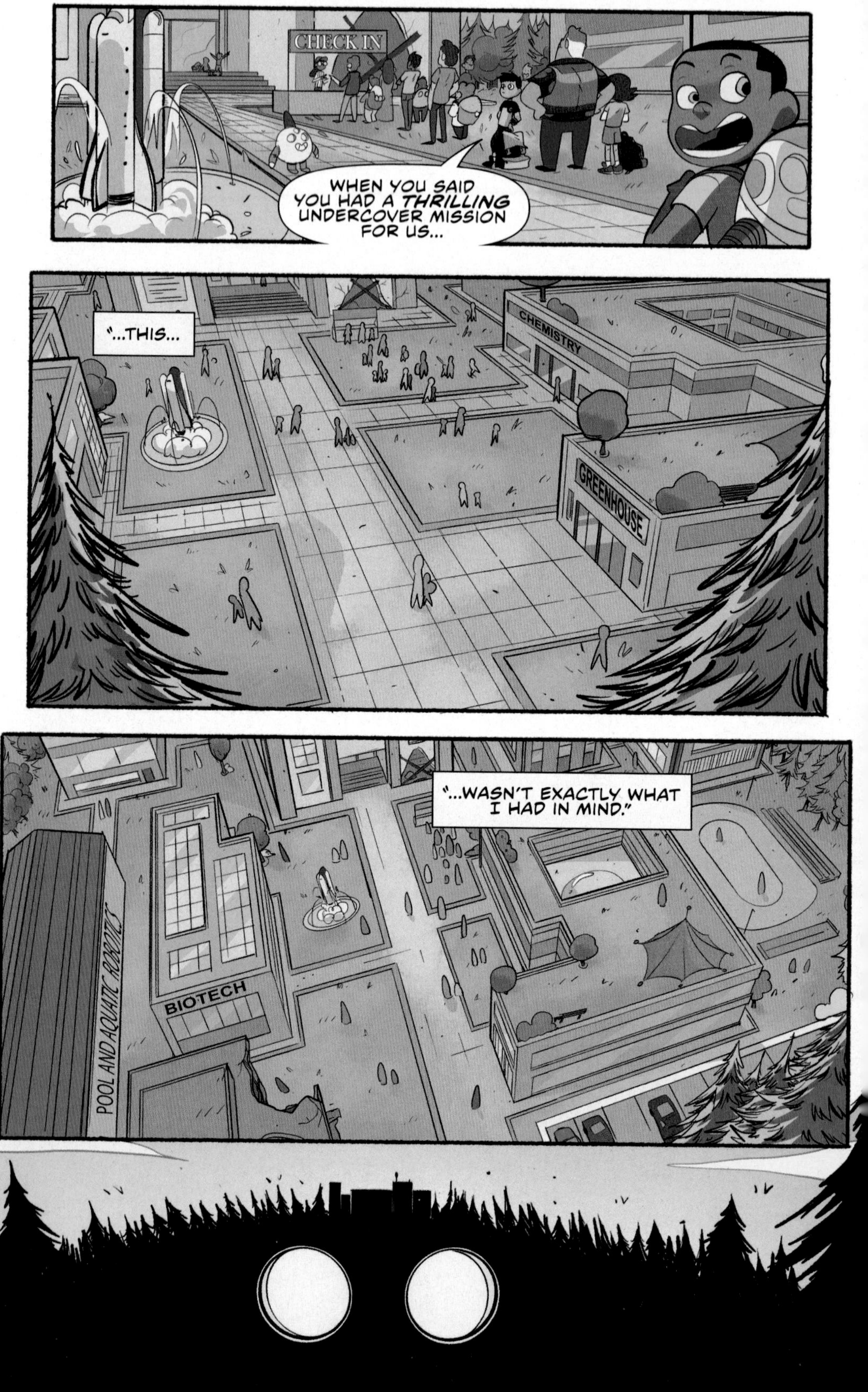
CHECK IN
WHEN YOU SAID YOU HAD A *THRILLING* UNDERCOVER MISSION FOR US...
"...THIS...
CHEMISTRY
GREENHOUSE
"...WASN'T EXACTLY WHAT I HAD IN MIND."
POOL AND AQUATIC ROBOTICS
BIOTECH

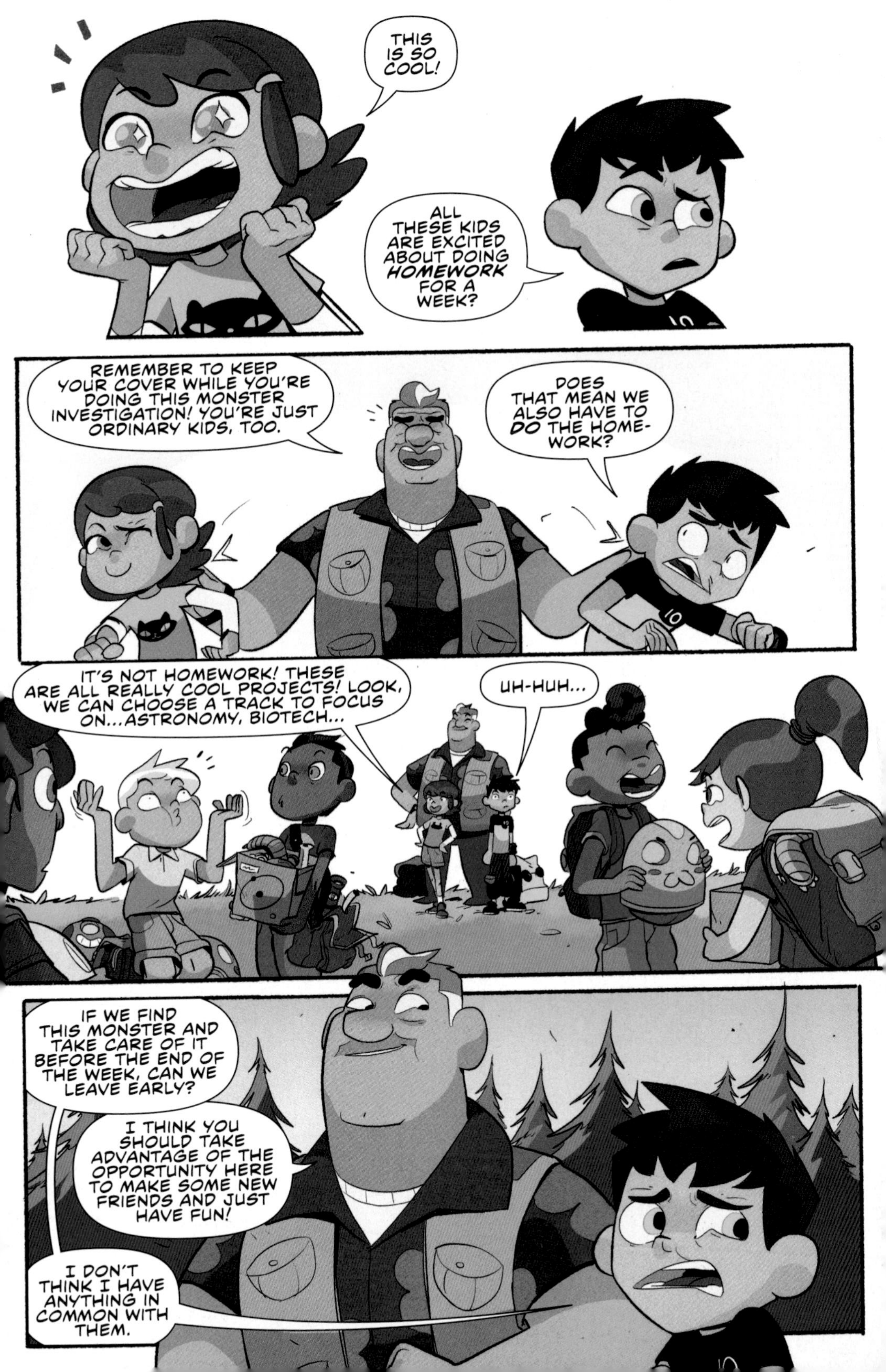
THIS IS SO COOL!
ALL THESE KIDS ARE EXCITED ABOUT DOING *HOMEWORK* FOR A WEEK?
REMEMBER TO KEEP YOUR COVER WHILE YOU'RE DOING THIS MONSTER INVESTIGATION! YOU'RE JUST ORDINARY KIDS, TOO.
DOES THAT MEAN WE ALSO HAVE TO *DO* THE HOME-WORK?
IT'S NOT HOMEWORK! THESE ARE ALL REALLY COOL PROJECTS! LOOK, WE CAN CHOOSE A TRACK TO FOCUS ON...ASTRONOMY, BIOTECH...
UH-HUH...
IF WE FIND THIS MONSTER AND TAKE CARE OF IT BEFORE THE END OF THE WEEK, CAN WE LEAVE EARLY?
I THINK YOU SHOULD TAKE ADVANTAGE OF THE OPPORTUNITY HERE TO MAKE SOME NEW FRIENDS AND JUST HAVE FUN!
I DON'T THINK I HAVE ANYTHING IN COMMON WITH THEM.

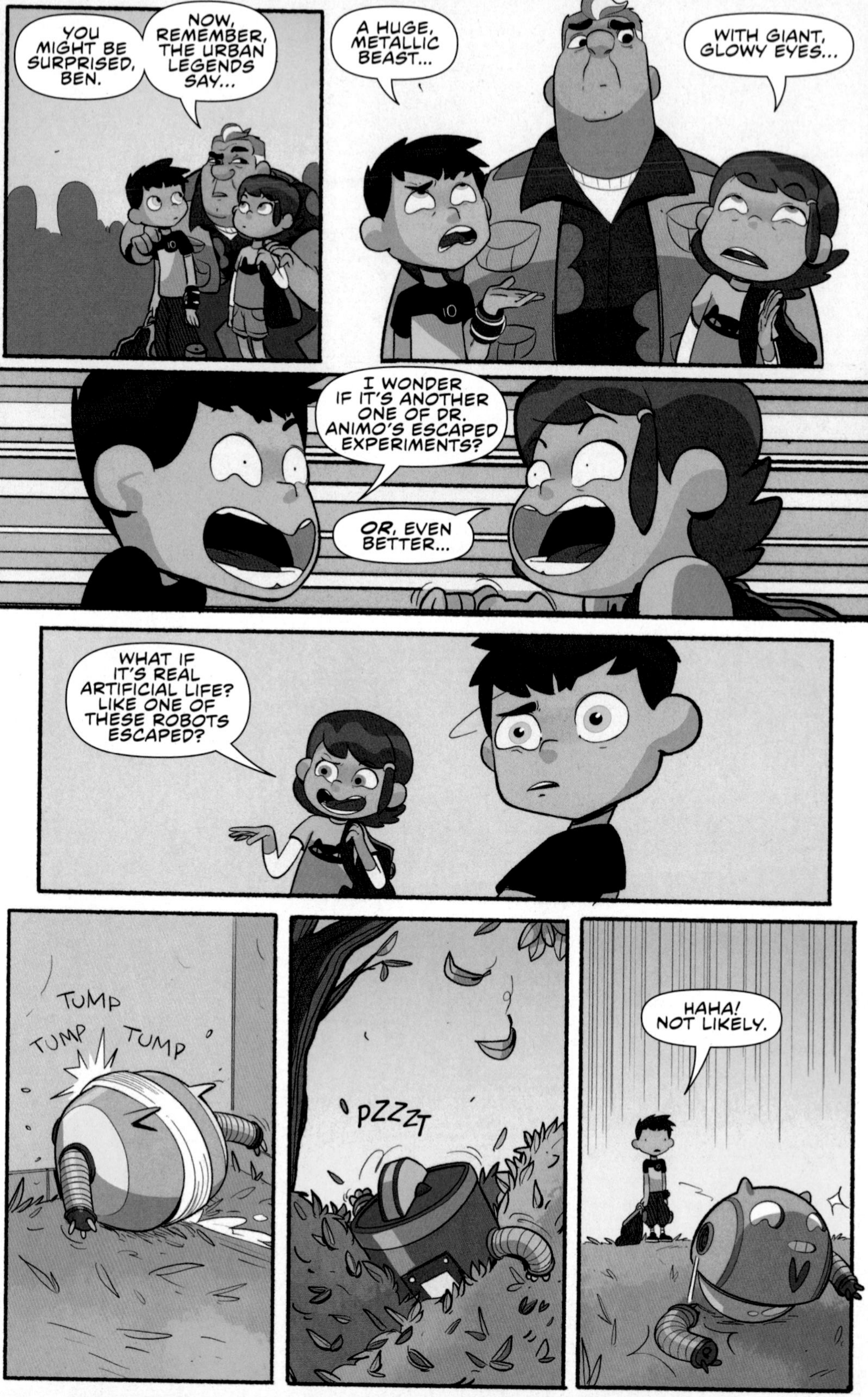
YOU MIGHT BE SURPRISED, BEN.
NOW, REMEMBER, THE URBAN LEGENDS SAY...
A HUGE, METALLIC BEAST...
WITH GIANT, GLOWY EYES...
I WONDER IF IT'S ANOTHER ONE OF DR. ANIMO'S ESCAPED EXPERIMENTS?
OR, EVEN BETTER...
WHAT IF IT'S REAL ARTIFICIAL LIFE? LIKE ONE OF THESE ROBOTS ESCAPED?
TUMP
TUMP TUMP
PZZZT
HAHA! NOT LIKELY.

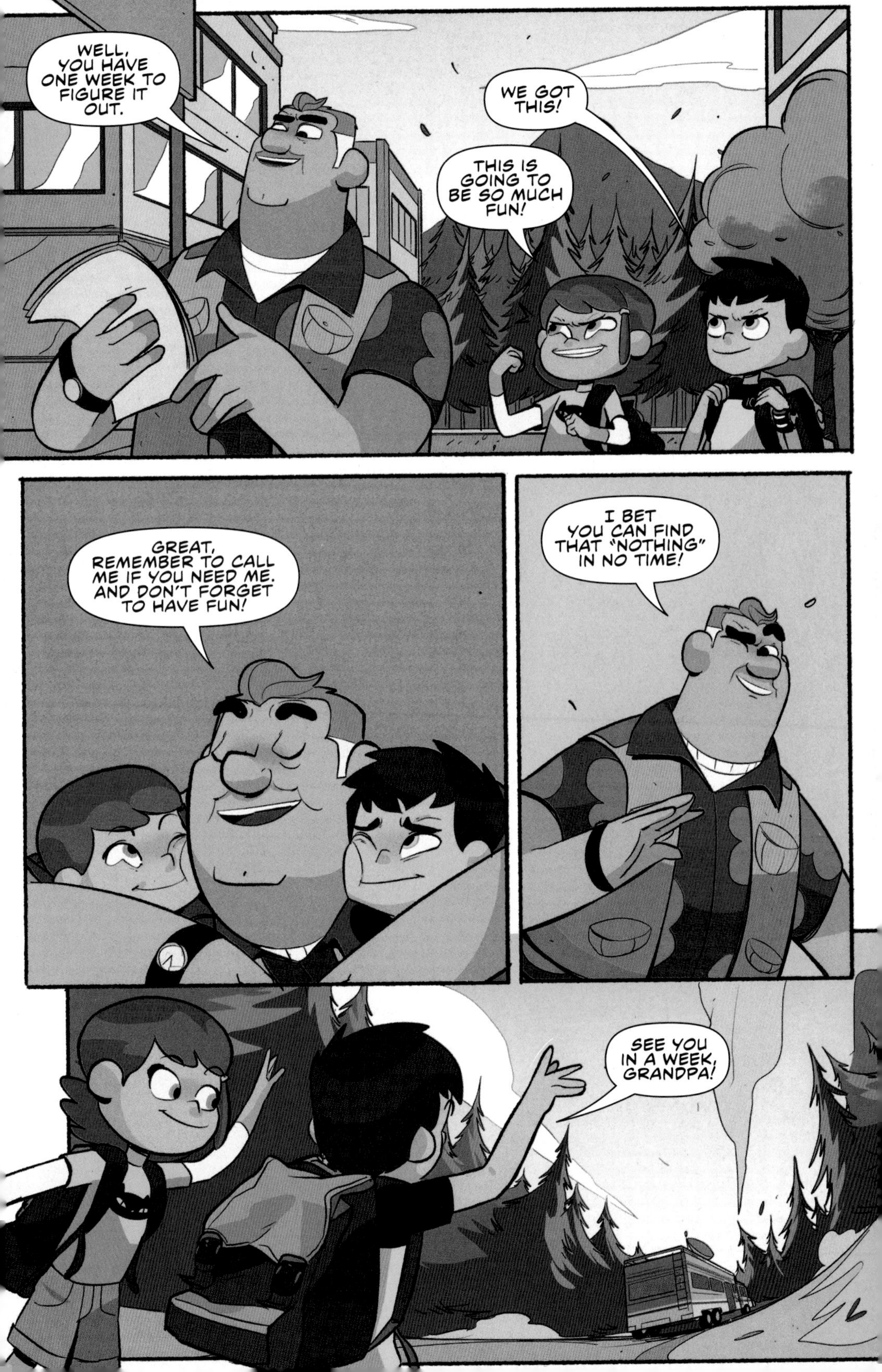
WELL, YOU HAVE ONE WEEK TO FIGURE IT OUT.
WE GOT THIS!
THIS IS GOING TO BE SO MUCH FUN!
GREAT, REMEMBER TO CALL ME IF YOU NEED ME. AND DON'T FORGET TO HAVE FUN!
I BET YOU CAN FIND THAT "NOTHING" IN NO TIME!
SEE YOU IN A WEEK, GRANDPA!

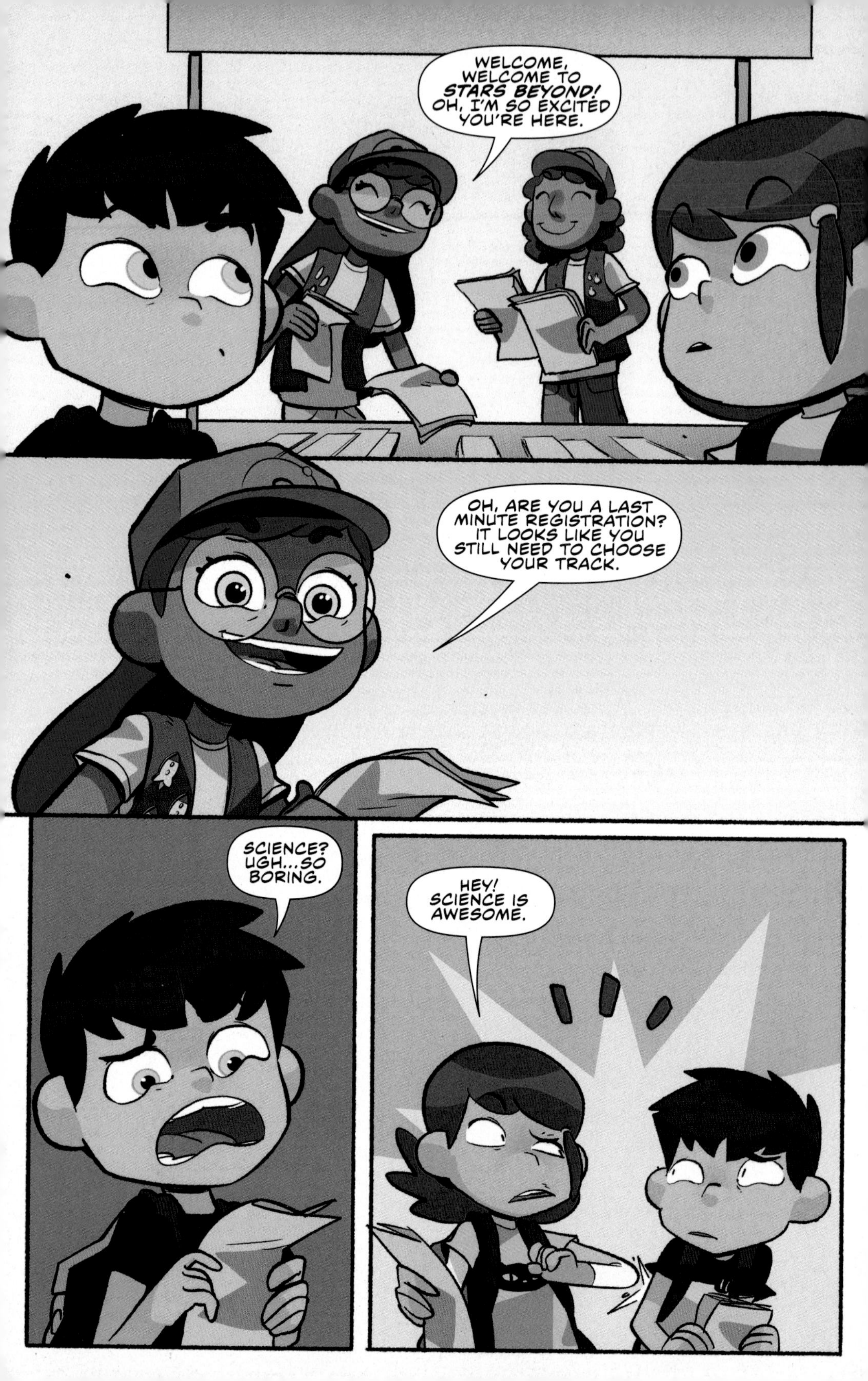
WELCOME, WELCOME TO STARS BEYOND! OH, I'M SO EXCITED YOU'RE HERE.
OH, ARE YOU A LAST MINUTE REGISTRATION? IT LOOKS LIKE YOU STILL NEED TO CHOOSE YOUR TRACK.
SCIENCE? UGH...SO BORING.
HEY! SCIENCE IS AWESOME.

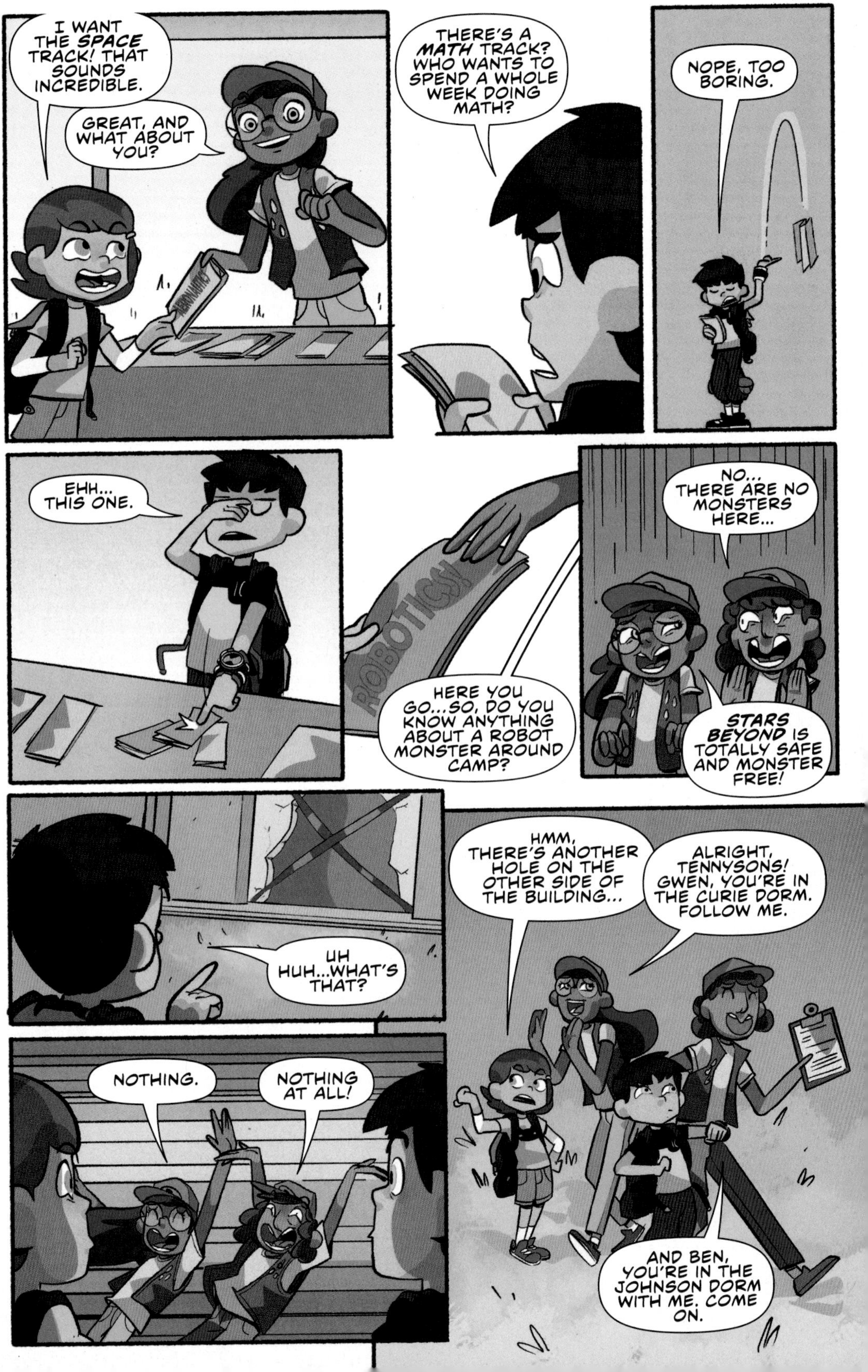
I WANT THE *SPACE* TRACK! THAT SOUNDS INCREDIBLE.
GREAT, AND WHAT ABOUT YOU?
THERE'S A *MATH* TRACK? WHO WANTS TO SPEND A WHOLE WEEK DOING MATH?
NOPE, TOO BORING.
EHH... THIS ONE.
ROBOTICS!
HERE YOU GO...SO, DO YOU KNOW ANYTHING ABOUT A ROBOT MONSTER AROUND CAMP?
NO... THERE ARE NO MONSTERS HERE...
STARS BEYOND IS TOTALLY SAFE AND MONSTER FREE!
UH HUH...WHAT'S THAT?
NOTHING.
NOTHING AT ALL!
HMM, THERE'S ANOTHER HOLE ON THE OTHER SIDE OF THE BUILDING...
ALRIGHT, TENNYSONS! GWEN, YOU'RE IN THE CURIE DORM. FOLLOW ME.
AND BEN, YOU'RE IN THE JOHNSON DORM WITH ME. COME ON.

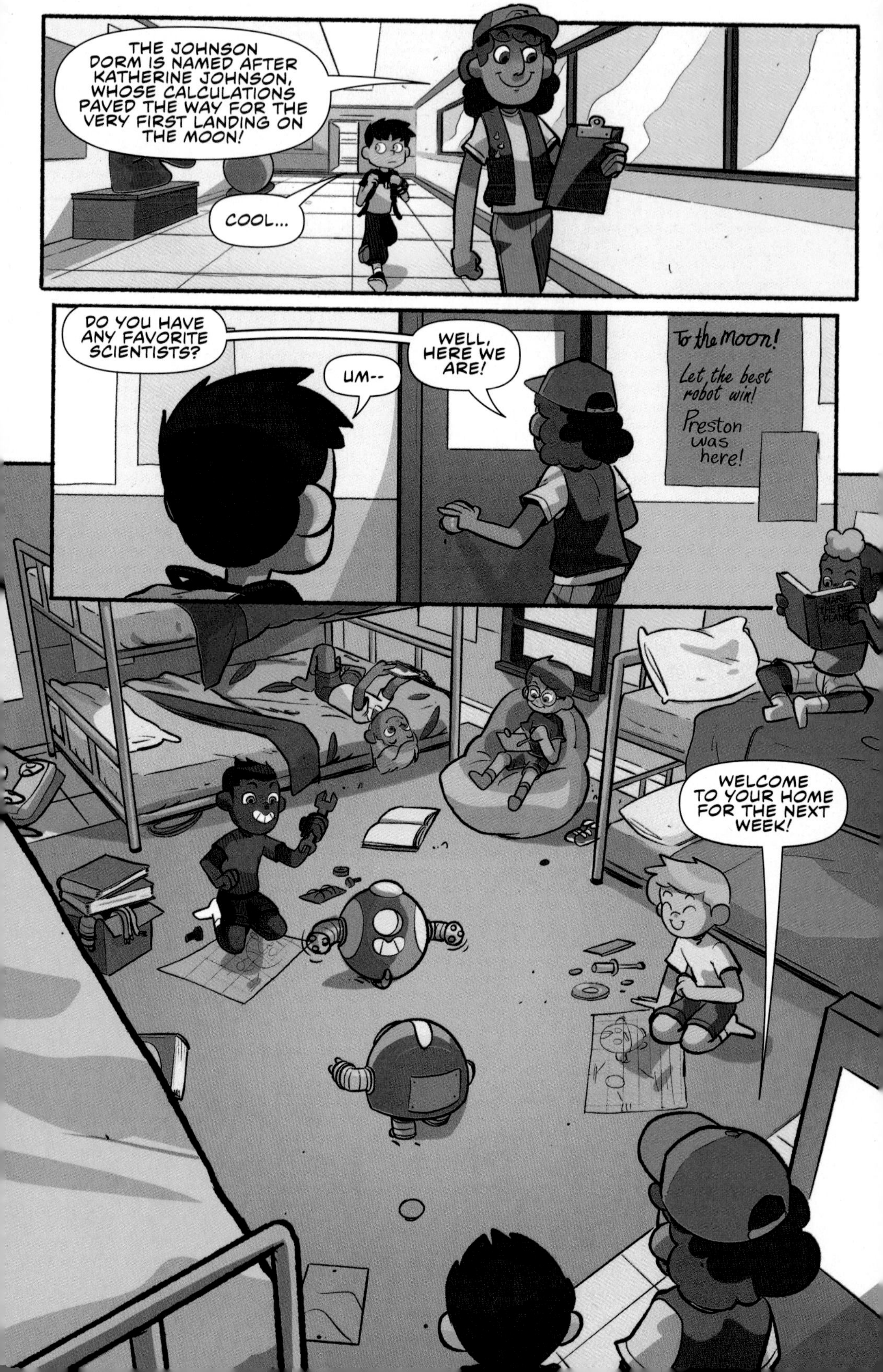
THE JOHNSON DORM IS NAMED AFTER KATHERINE JOHNSON, WHOSE CALCULATIONS PAVED THE WAY FOR THE VERY FIRST LANDING ON THE MOON!
COOL...
DO YOU HAVE ANY FAVORITE SCIENTISTS?
UM--
WELL, HERE WE ARE!
To the moon!
Let the best robot win!
Preston was here!
WELCOME TO YOUR HOME FOR THE NEXT WEEK!

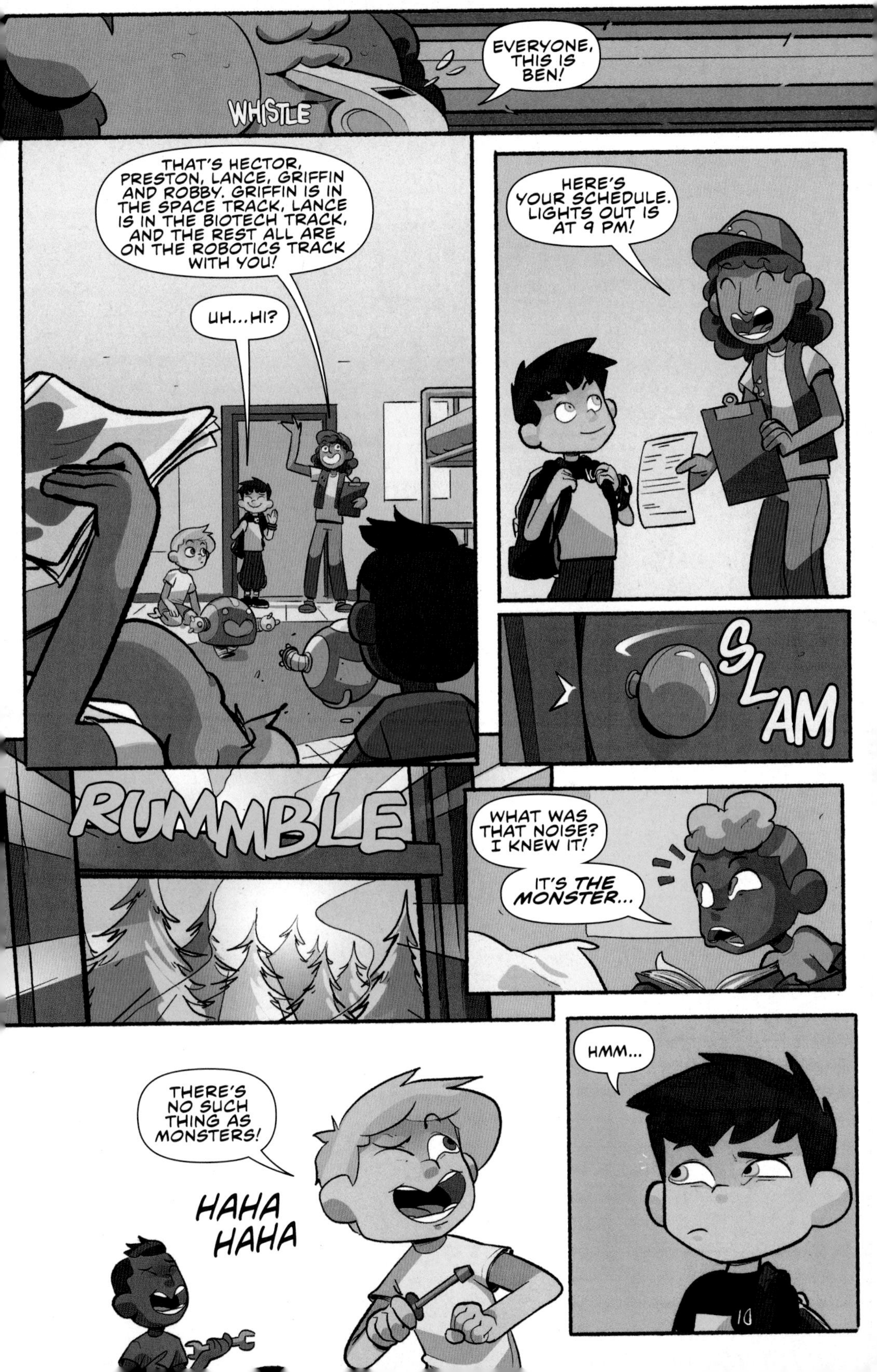

WHISTLE
EVERYONE, THIS IS BEN!
THAT'S HECTOR, PRESTON, LANCE, GRIFFIN AND ROBBY. GRIFFIN IS IN THE SPACE TRACK, LANCE IS IN THE BIOTECH TRACK, AND THE REST ALL ARE ON THE ROBOTICS TRACK WITH YOU!
UH...HI?
HERE'S YOUR SCHEDULE. LIGHTS OUT IS AT 9 PM!
SLAM
RUMMBLE
WHAT WAS THAT NOISE? I KNEW IT!
IT'S THE MONSTER...
THERE'S NO SUCH THING AS MONSTERS!
HAHA HAHA
HMM...

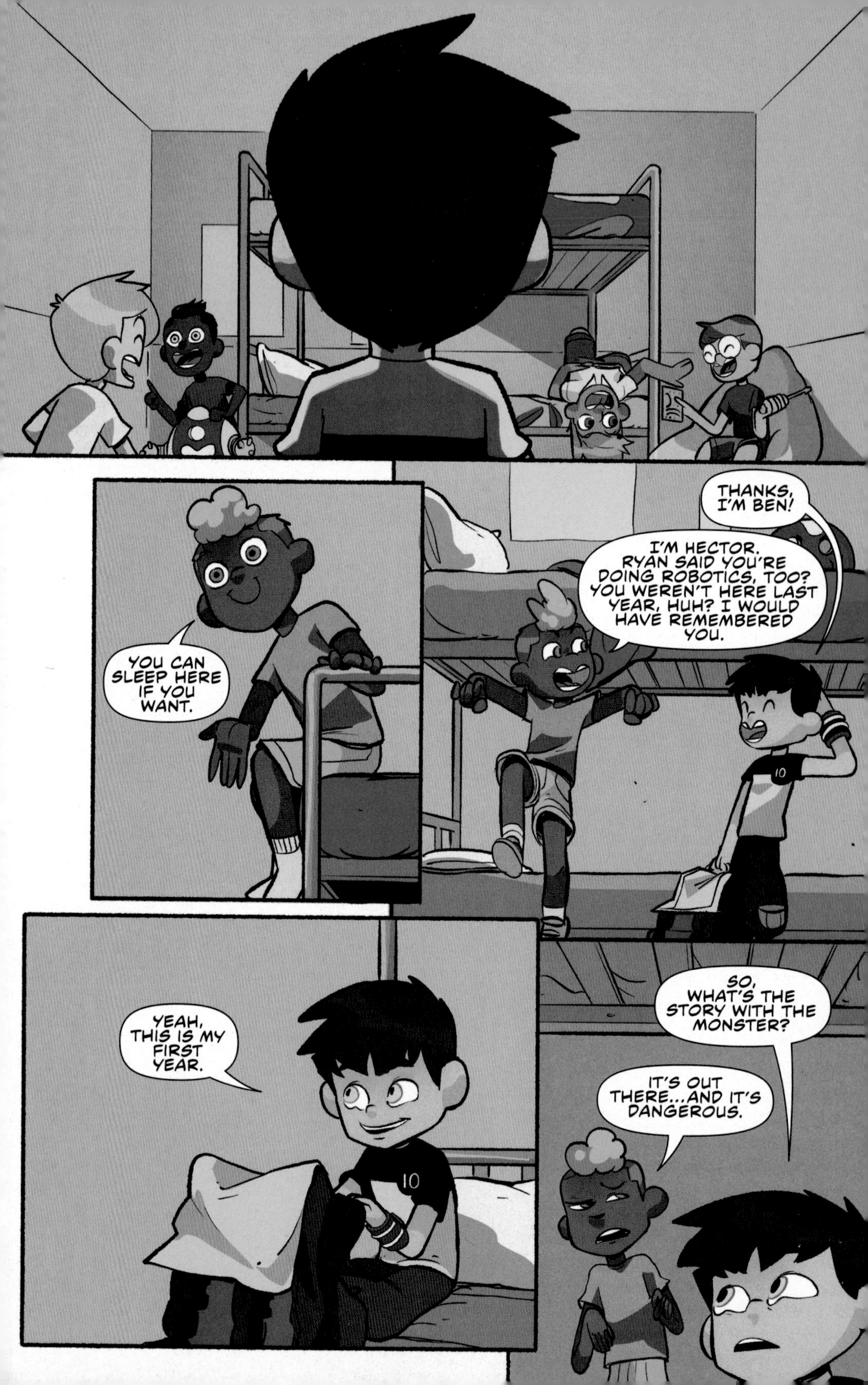
YOU CAN SLEEP HERE IF YOU WANT.
THANKS, I'M BEN!
I'M HECTOR. RYAN SAID YOU'RE DOING ROBOTICS, TOO? YOU WEREN'T HERE LAST YEAR, HUH? I WOULD HAVE REMEMBERED YOU.
YEAH, THIS IS MY FIRST YEAR.
SO, WHAT'S THE STORY WITH THE MONSTER?
IT'S OUT THERE...AND IT'S DANGEROUS.
10

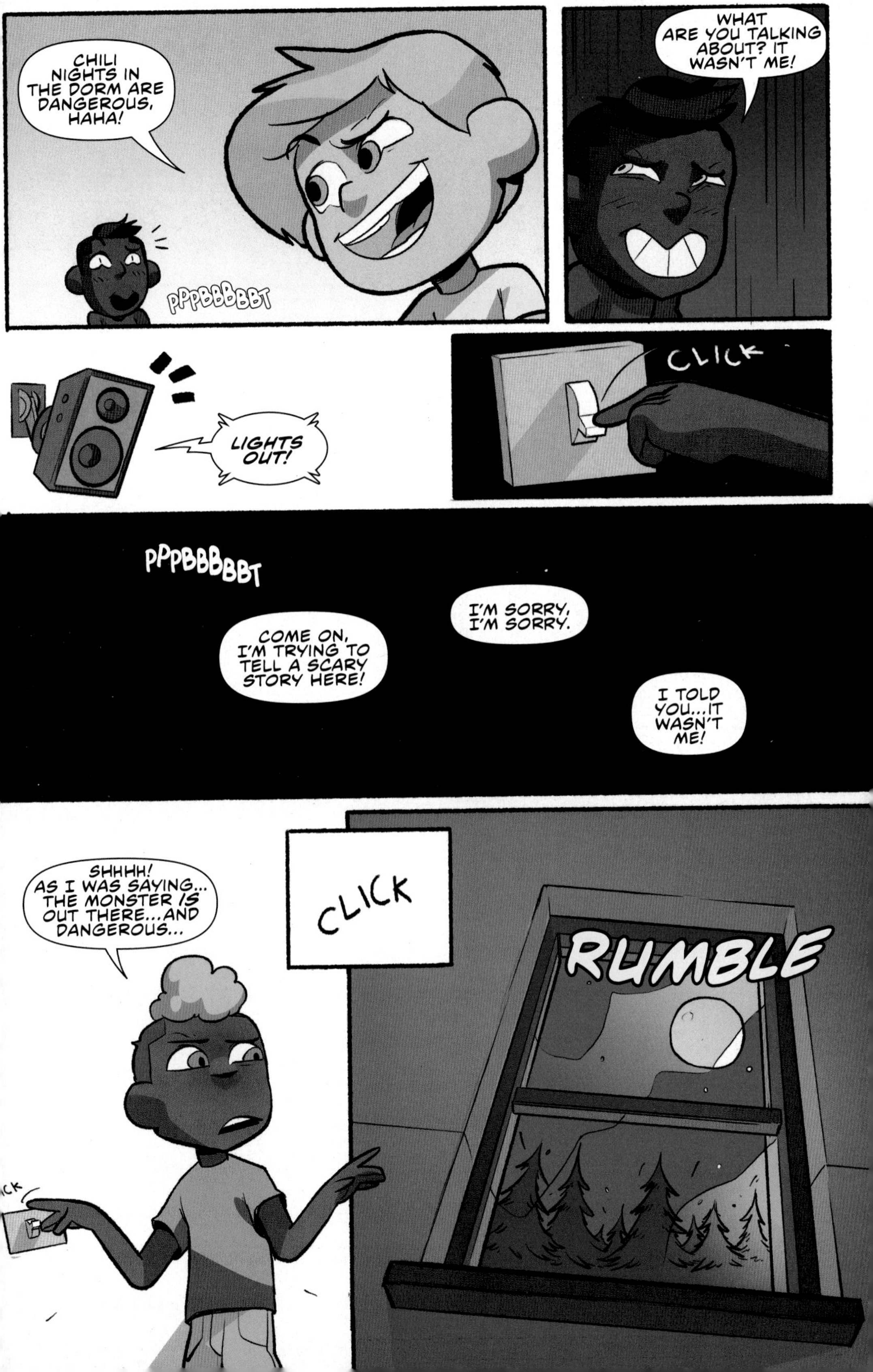
CHILI NIGHTS IN THE DORM ARE DANGEROUS, HAHA!
PPPBBBBBT
WHAT ARE YOU TALKING ABOUT? IT WASN'T ME!
LIGHTS OUT!
CLICK
PPPBBBBBT
COME ON, I'M TRYING TO TELL A SCARY STORY HERE!
I'M SORRY, I'M SORRY.
I TOLD YOU...IT WASN'T ME!
SHHHH! AS I WAS SAYING... THE MONSTER IS OUT THERE...AND DANGEROUS...
CLICK
RUMBLE

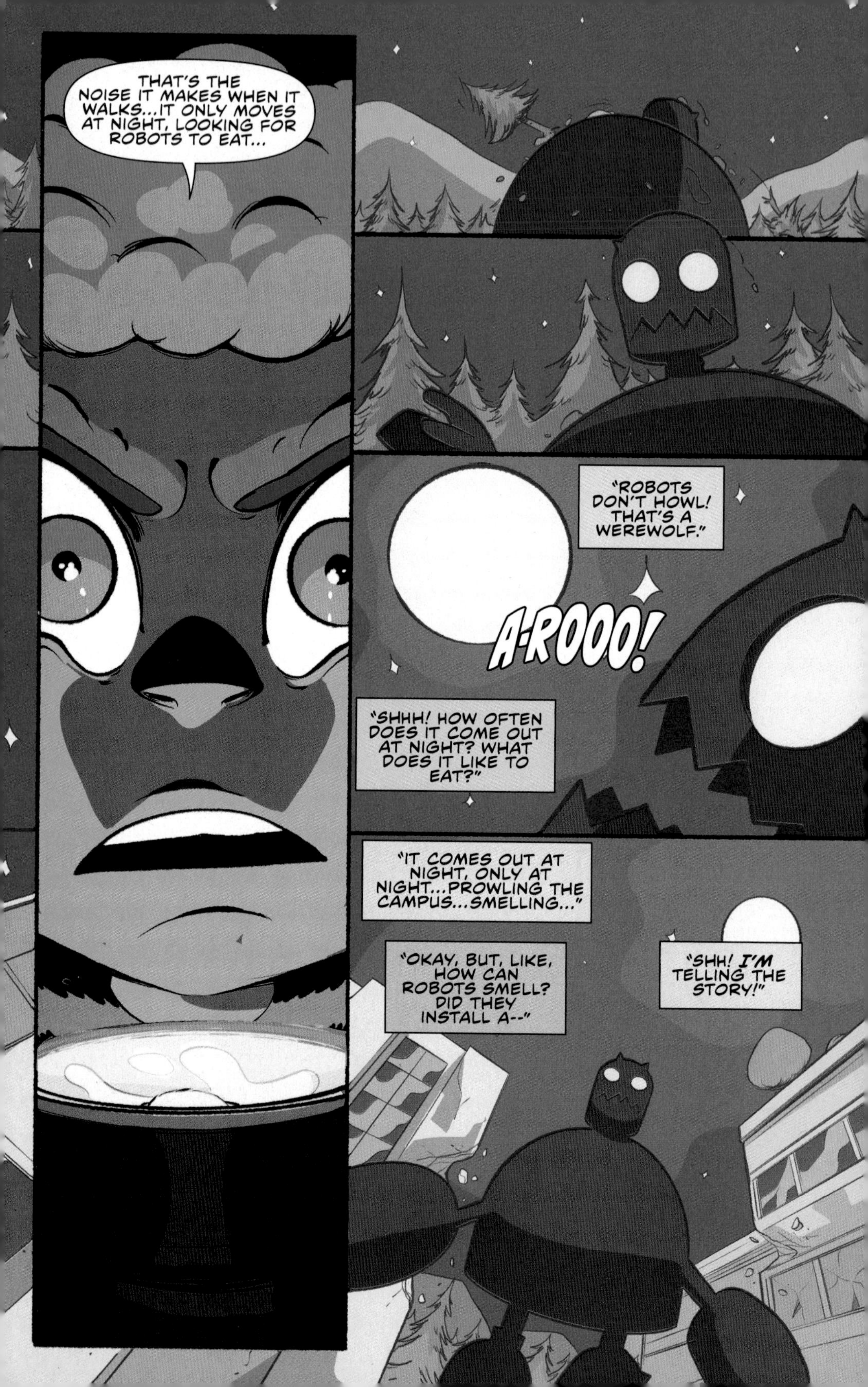

THAT'S THE NOISE IT MAKES WHEN IT WALKS...IT ONLY MOVES AT NIGHT, LOOKING FOR ROBOTS TO EAT...
"ROBOTS DON'T HOWL! THAT'S A WEREWOLF."
A-ROOO!
"SHHH! HOW OFTEN DOES IT COME OUT AT NIGHT? WHAT DOES IT LIKE TO EAT?"
"IT COMES OUT AT NIGHT, ONLY AT NIGHT...PROWLING THE CAMPUS...SMELLING..."
"OKAY, BUT, LIKE, HOW CAN ROBOTS SMELL? DID THEY INSTALL A--"
"SHH! *I'M* TELLING THE STORY!"

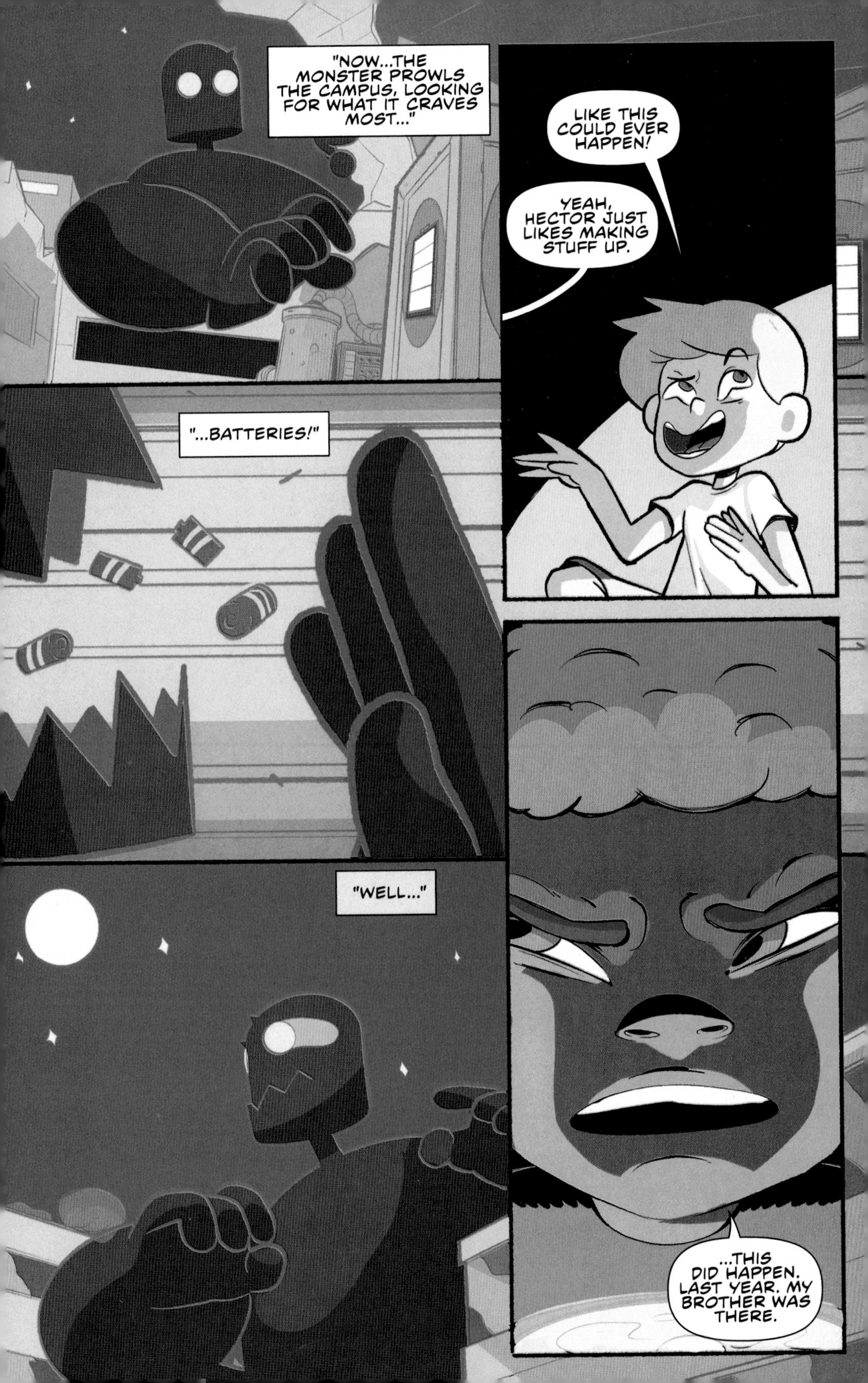
"NOW...THE MONSTER PROWLS THE CAMPUS, LOOKING FOR WHAT IT CRAVES MOST..."
LIKE THIS COULD EVER HAPPEN!
YEAH, HECTOR JUST LIKES MAKING STUFF UP.
"...BATTERIES!"
"WELL..."
...THIS DID HAPPEN. LAST YEAR. MY BROTHER WAS THERE.

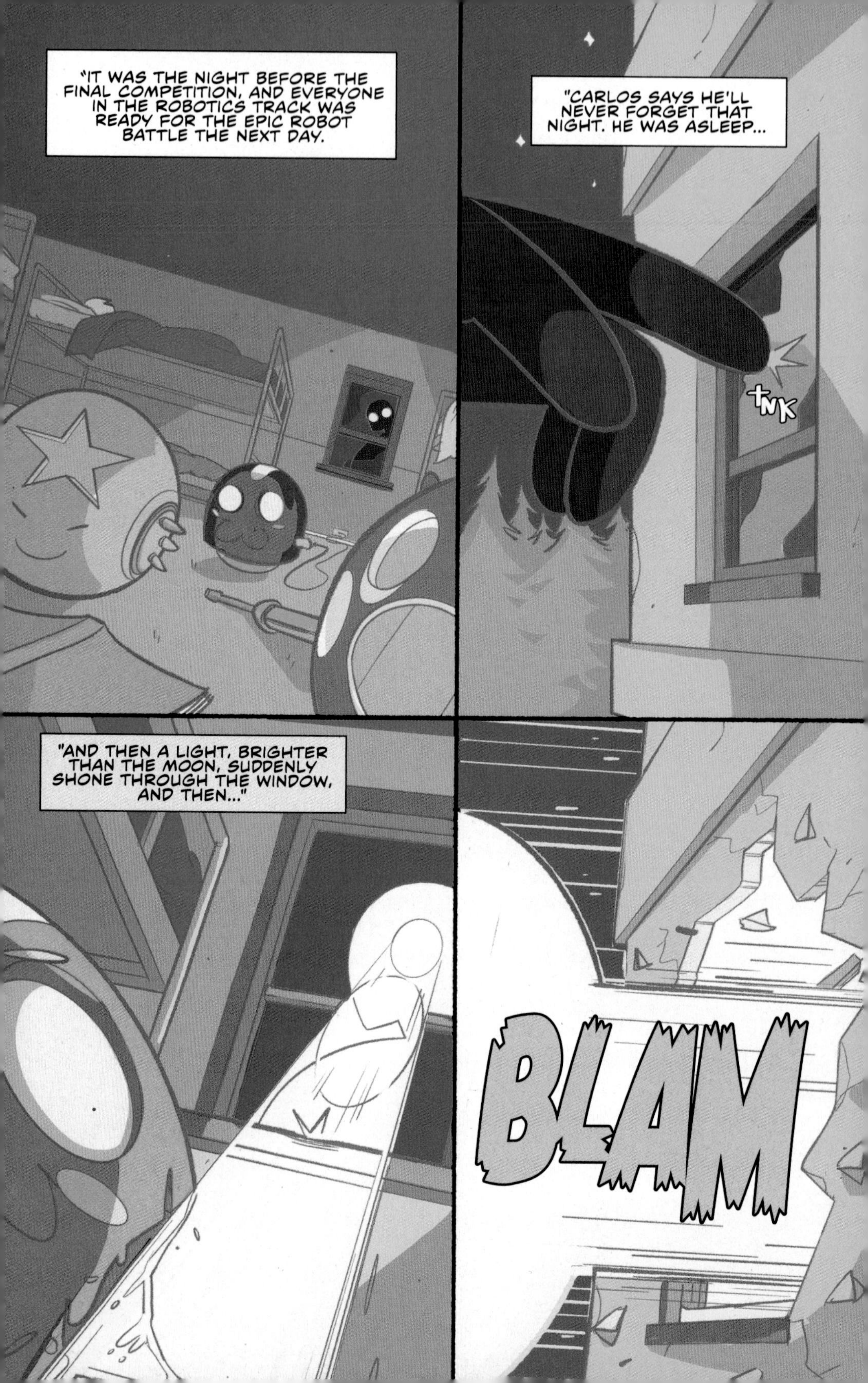
"IT WAS THE NIGHT BEFORE THE FINAL COMPETITION, AND EVERYONE IN THE ROBOTICS TRACK WAS READY FOR THE EPIC ROBOT BATTLE THE NEXT DAY.
"CARLOS SAYS HE'LL NEVER FORGET THAT NIGHT. HE WAS ASLEEP...
TNK
"AND THEN A LIGHT, BRIGHTER THAN THE MOON, SUDDENLY SHONE THROUGH THE WINDOW, AND THEN..."
BLAM

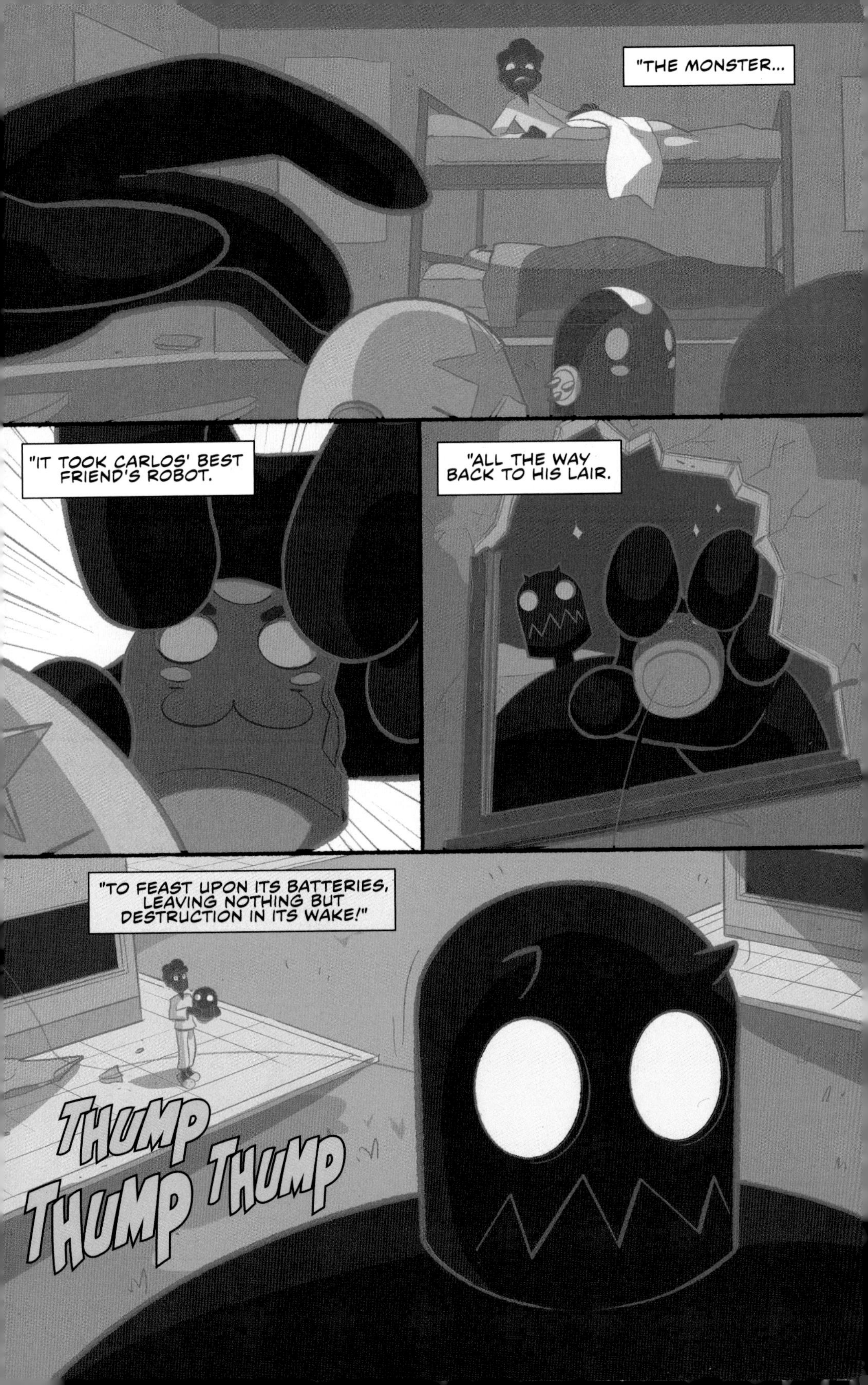
"THE MONSTER...
"IT TOOK CARLOS' BEST FRIEND'S ROBOT.
"ALL THE WAY BACK TO HIS LAIR.
"TO FEAST UPON ITS BATTERIES, LEAVING NOTHING BUT DESTRUCTION IN ITS WAKE!"
THUMP
THUMP THUMP

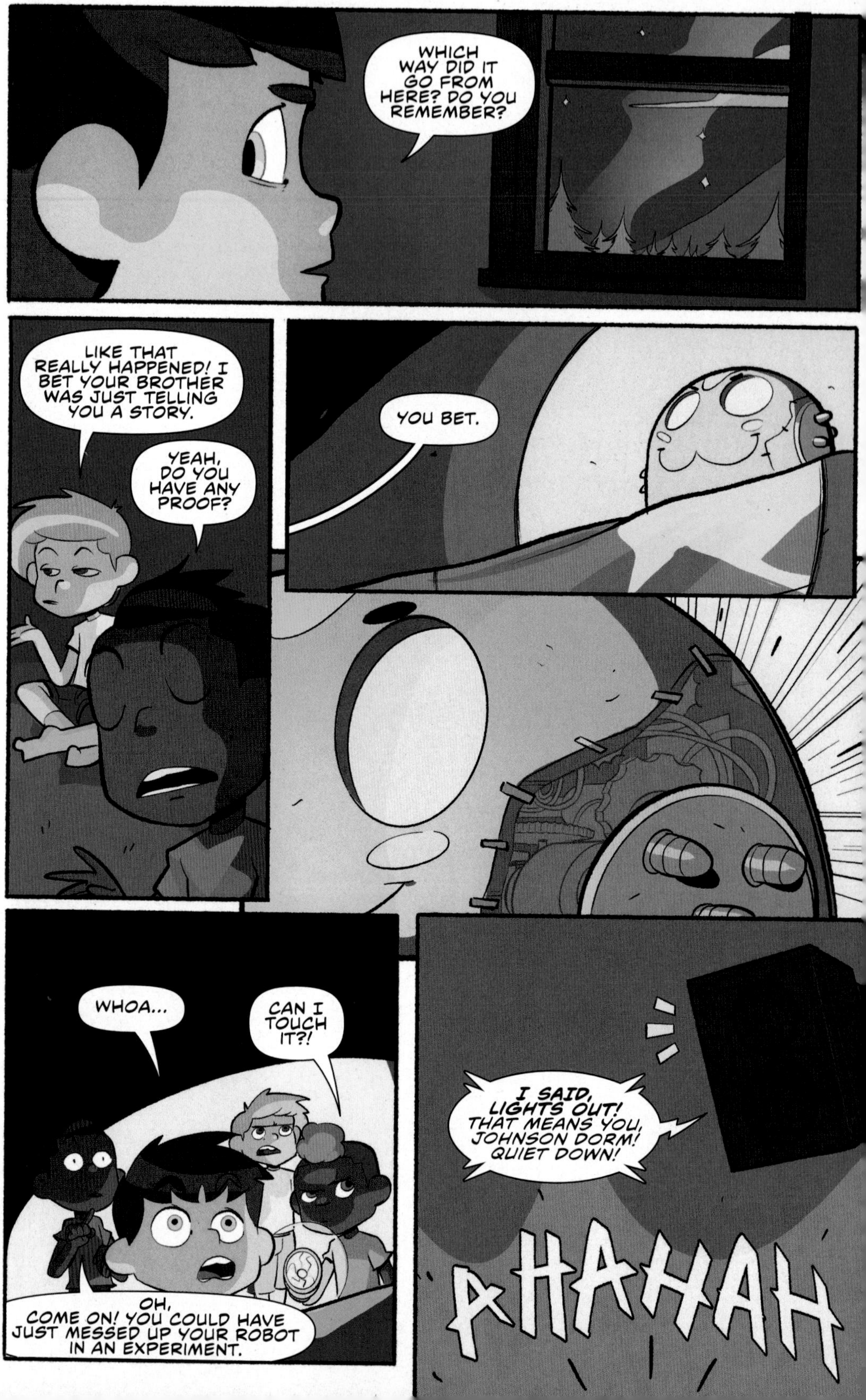
WHICH WAY DID IT GO FROM HERE? DO YOU REMEMBER?
LIKE THAT REALLY HAPPENED! I BET YOUR BROTHER WAS JUST TELLING YOU A STORY.
YEAH, DO YOU HAVE ANY PROOF?
YOU BET.
WHOA...
CAN I TOUCH IT?!
OH, COME ON! YOU COULD HAVE JUST MESSED UP YOUR ROBOT IN AN EXPERIMENT.
I SAID, LIGHTS OUT! THAT MEANS YOU, JOHNSON DORM! QUIET DOWN!
AHAHAH

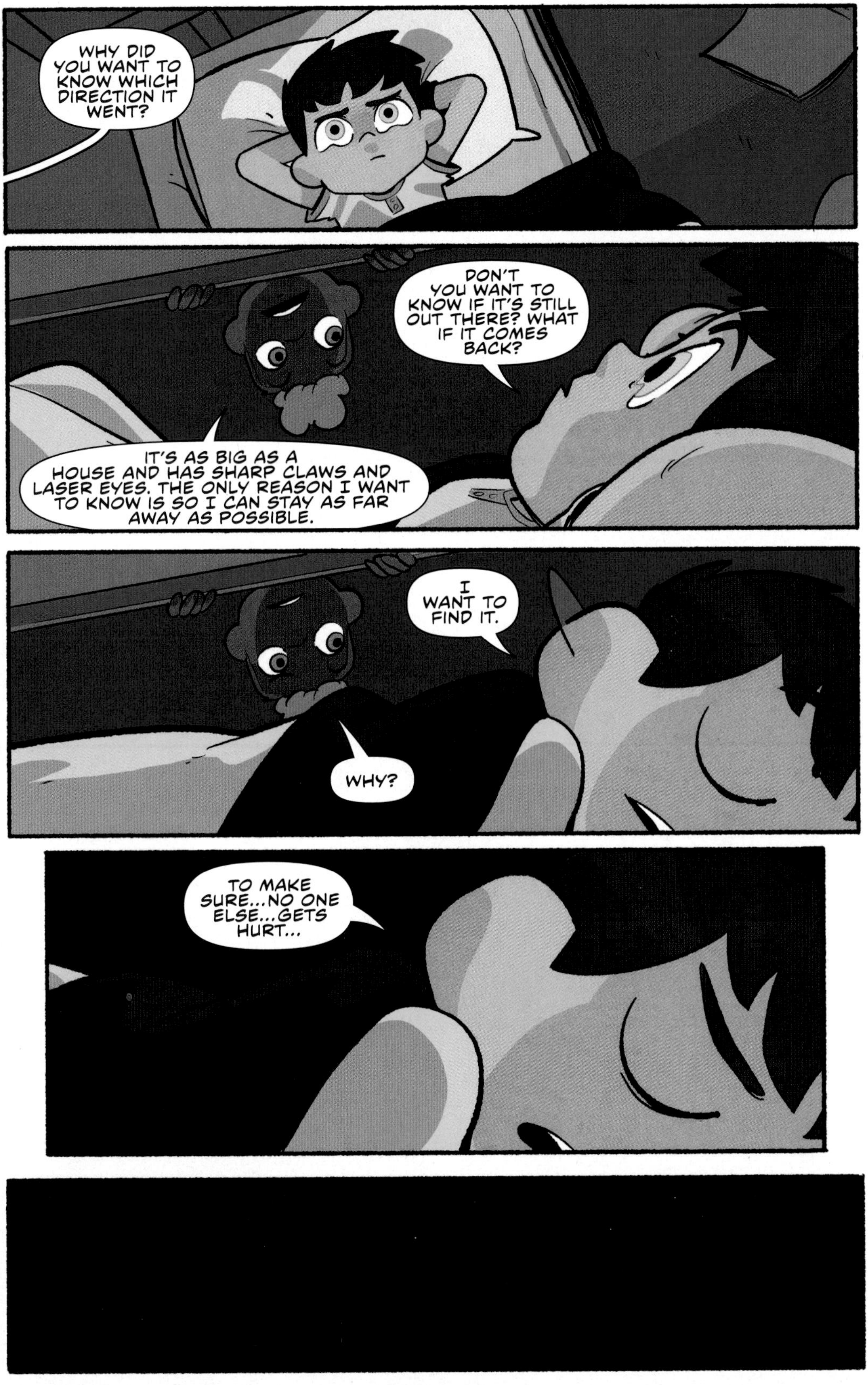
WHY DID YOU WANT TO KNOW WHICH DIRECTION IT WENT?
DON'T YOU WANT TO KNOW IF IT'S STILL OUT THERE? WHAT IF IT COMES BACK?
IT'S AS BIG AS A HOUSE AND HAS SHARP CLAWS AND LASER EYES. THE ONLY REASON I WANT TO KNOW IS SO I CAN STAY AS FAR AWAY AS POSSIBLE.
I WANT TO FIND IT.
WHY?
TO MAKE SURE...NO ONE ELSE...GETS HURT...

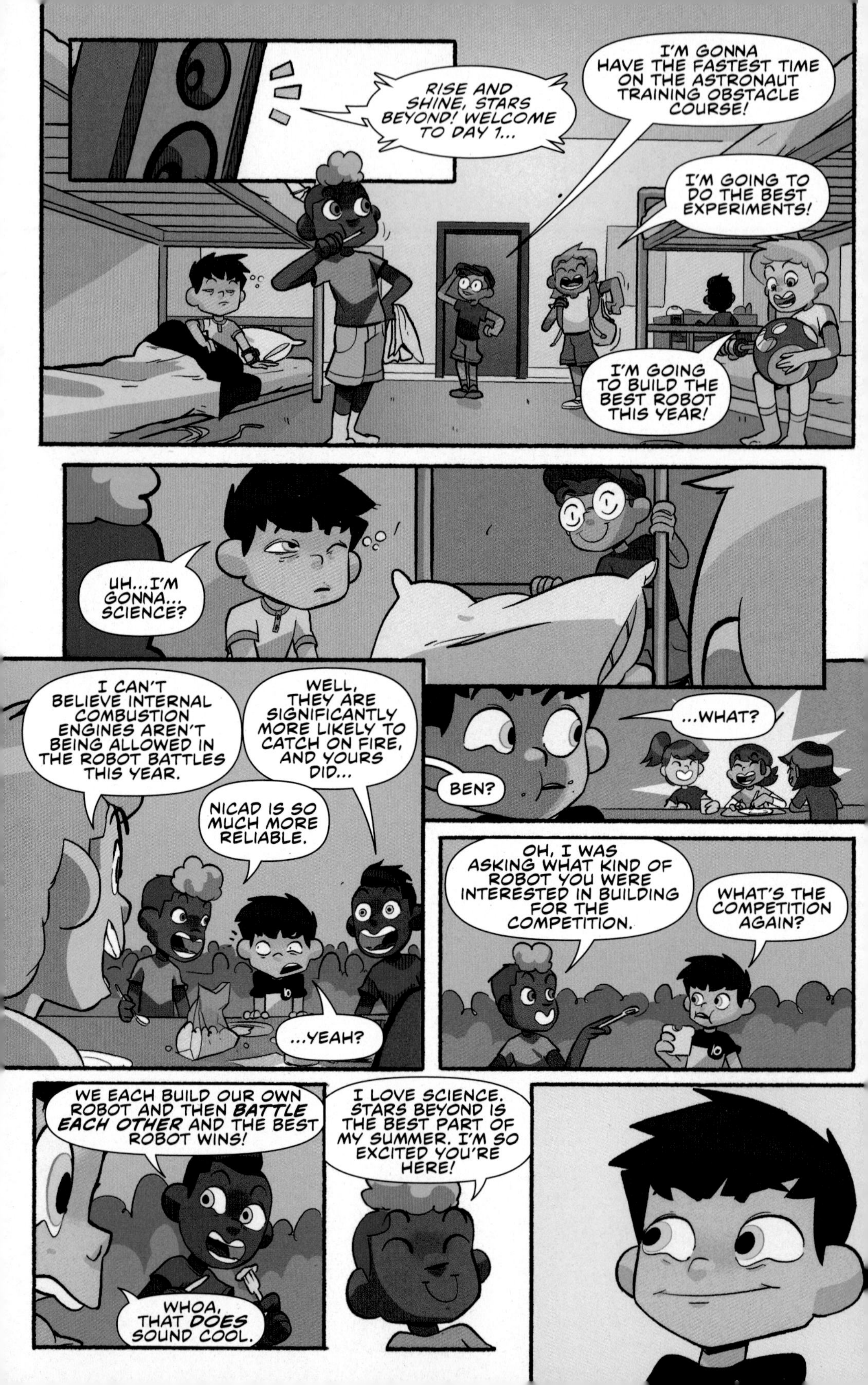
RISE AND SHINE, STARS BEYOND! WELCOME TO DAY 1...
I'M GONNA HAVE THE FASTEST TIME ON THE ASTRONAUT TRAINING OBSTACLE COURSE!
I'M GOING TO DO THE BEST EXPERIMENTS!
I'M GOING TO BUILD THE BEST ROBOT THIS YEAR!
UH...I'M GONNA... SCIENCE?
I CAN'T BELIEVE INTERNAL COMBUSTION ENGINES AREN'T BEING ALLOWED IN THE ROBOT BATTLES THIS YEAR.
WELL, THEY ARE SIGNIFICANTLY MORE LIKELY TO CATCH ON FIRE, AND YOURS DID...
NICAD IS SO MUCH MORE RELIABLE.
...YEAH?
...WHAT?
BEN?
OH, I WAS ASKING WHAT KIND OF ROBOT YOU WERE INTERESTED IN BUILDING FOR THE COMPETITION.
WHAT'S THE COMPETITION AGAIN?
WE EACH BUILD OUR OWN ROBOT AND THEN *BATTLE EACH OTHER* AND THE BEST ROBOT WINS!
WHOA, THAT *DOES* SOUND COOL.
I LOVE SCIENCE. STARS BEYOND IS THE BEST PART OF MY SUMMER. I'M SO EXCITED YOU'RE HERE!

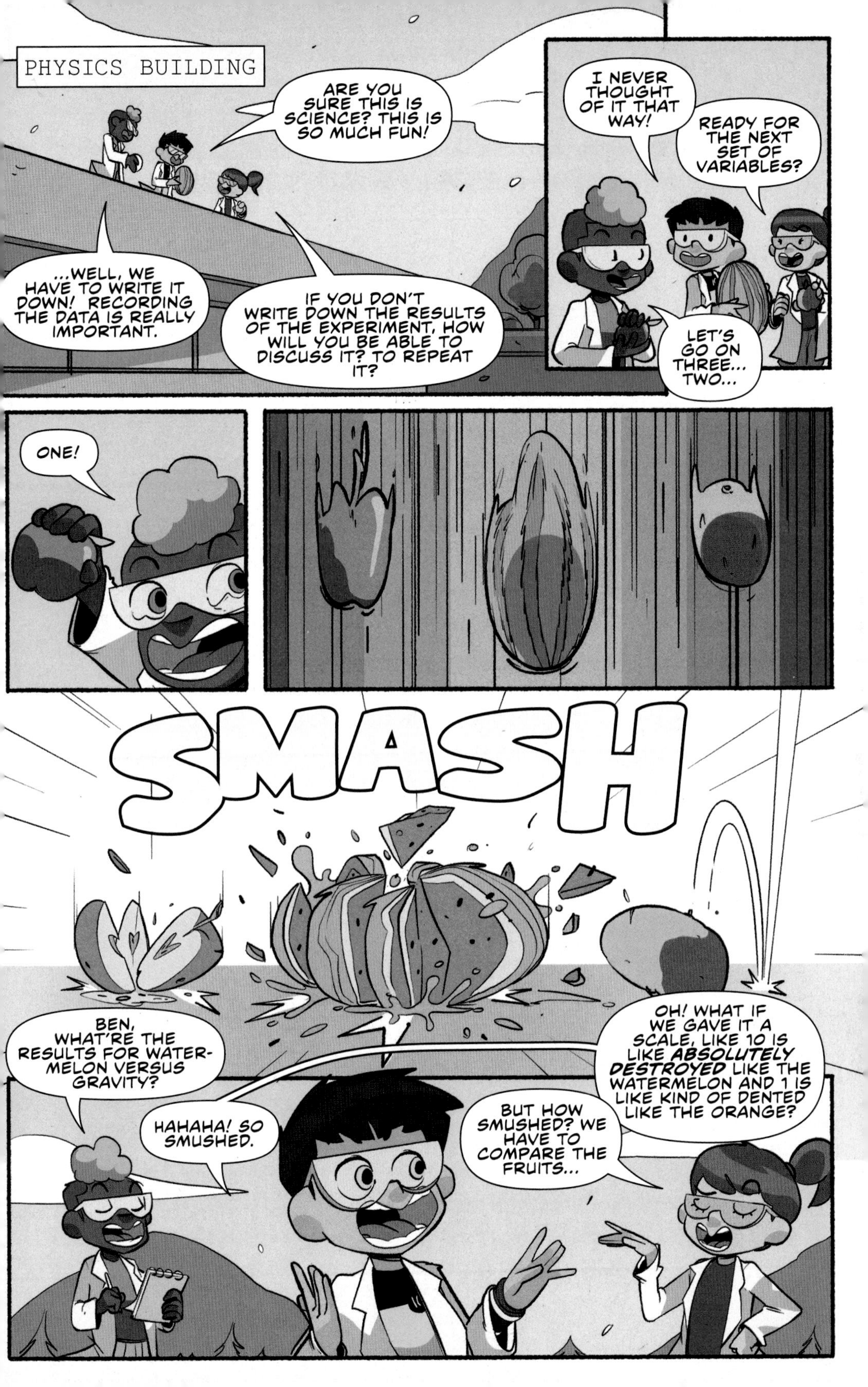
PHYSICS BUILDING
ARE YOU SURE THIS IS SCIENCE? THIS IS SO MUCH FUN!
...WELL, WE HAVE TO WRITE IT DOWN! RECORDING THE DATA IS REALLY IMPORTANT.
IF YOU DON'T WRITE DOWN THE RESULTS OF THE EXPERIMENT, HOW WILL YOU BE ABLE TO DISCUSS IT? TO REPEAT IT?
I NEVER THOUGHT OF IT THAT WAY!
READY FOR THE NEXT SET OF VARIABLES?
LET'S GO ON THREE... TWO...
ONE!
SMASH
BEN, WHAT'RE THE RESULTS FOR WATER-MELON VERSUS GRAVITY?
HAHAHA! SO SMUSHED.
BUT HOW SMUSHED? WE HAVE TO COMPARE THE FRUITS...
OH! WHAT IF WE GAVE IT A SCALE, LIKE 10 IS LIKE ***ABSOLUTELY DESTROYED*** LIKE THE WATERMELON AND 1 IS LIKE KIND OF DENTED LIKE THE ORANGE?

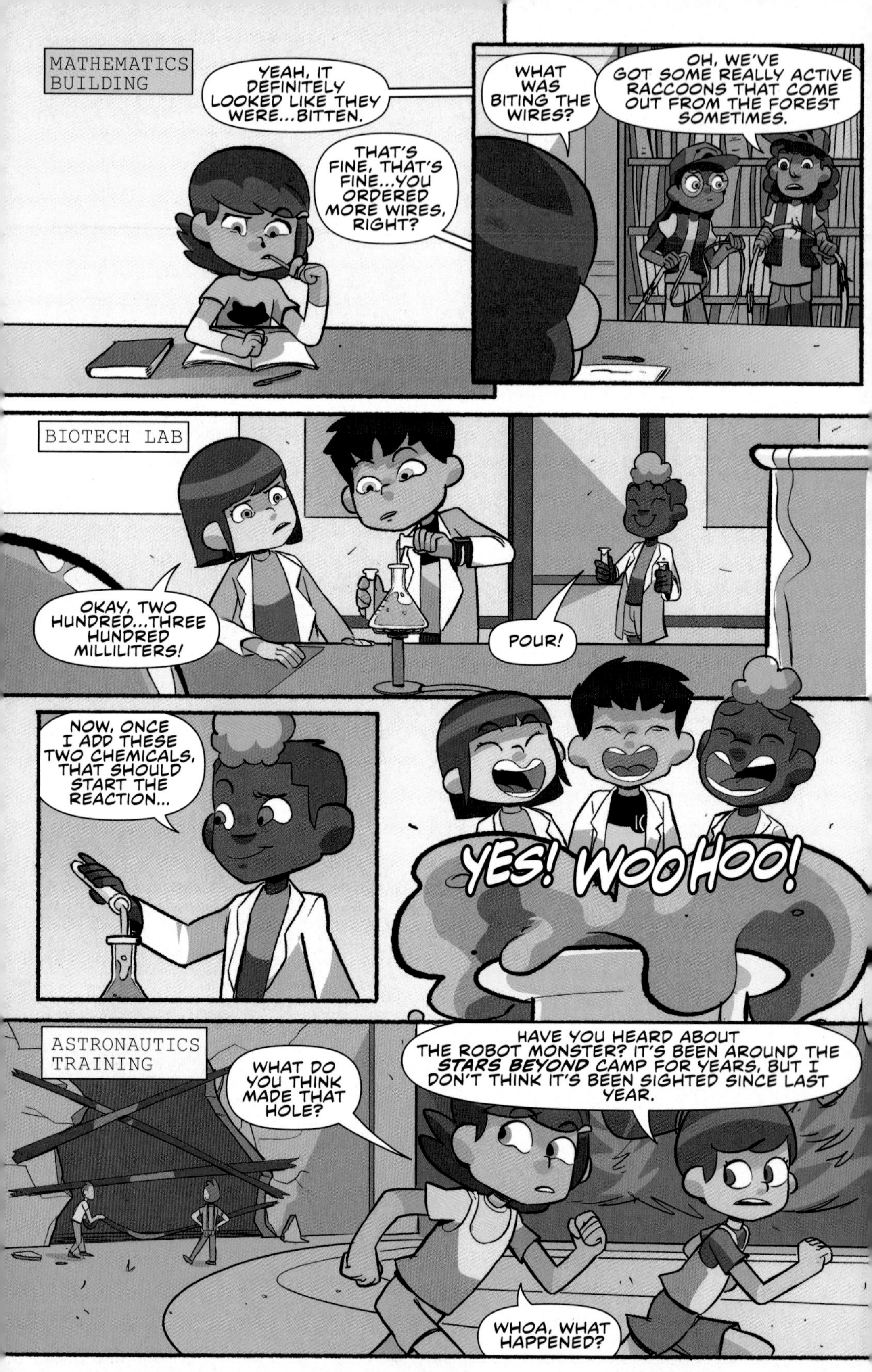
MATHEMATICS BUILDING
YEAH, IT DEFINITELY LOOKED LIKE THEY WERE...BITTEN.
THAT'S FINE, THAT'S FINE...YOU ORDERED MORE WIRES, RIGHT?
WHAT WAS BITING THE WIRES?
OH, WE'VE GOT SOME REALLY ACTIVE RACCOONS THAT COME OUT FROM THE FOREST SOMETIMES.
BIOTECH LAB
OKAY, TWO HUNDRED...THREE HUNDRED MILLILITERS!
POUR!
NOW, ONCE I ADD THESE TWO CHEMICALS, THAT SHOULD START THE REACTION...
YES! WOOHOO!
ASTRONAUTICS TRAINING
WHAT DO YOU THINK MADE THAT HOLE?
HAVE YOU HEARD ABOUT THE ROBOT MONSTER? IT'S BEEN AROUND THE *STARS BEYOND* CAMP FOR YEARS, BUT I DON'T THINK IT'S BEEN SIGHTED SINCE LAST YEAR.
WHOA, WHAT HAPPENED?

LATER...

BEN! DID YOU HEAR HOW THE ROBOT MONSTER STOLE A--

YEAH, YEAH, YEAH, HECTOR TOLD ME ALL ABOUT IT.

BUT WAIT, IF WE USE FM INSTEAD OF AM FOR OUR RADIO SIGNAL IT WOULD BE BETTER, RIGHT?

YEAH! THIS WAY OUR ROBOT WOULD BE SO MUCH--

--FASTER BECAUSE FM SIGNALS TRAVEL BETTER DURING THE DAY!

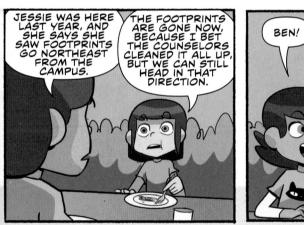

JESSIE WAS HERE LAST YEAR, AND SHE SAYS SHE SAW FOOTPRINTS GO NORTHEAST FROM THE CAMPUS.

THE FOOTPRINTS ARE GONE NOW, BECAUSE I BET THE COUNSELORS CLEANED IT ALL UP, BUT WE CAN STILL HEAD IN THAT DIRECTION.

BEN!

GWEN, COME ON! THIS IS REALLY COOL STUFF AND I NEVER GET TO HANG OUT WITH KIDS MY AGE LIKE THIS.

ALRIGHT, AFTER LUNCH LET'S GO CHECK IT OUT! WHO WANTS TO COME WITH ME? LET'S START IN THE CHEMISTRY BUILDING, BECAUSE THAT'S WHERE THAT HOLE IS...

SOUNDS COOL!

YEAH, THAT MUST BE WHERE THE MONSTER WAS LAST. LET'S GO!

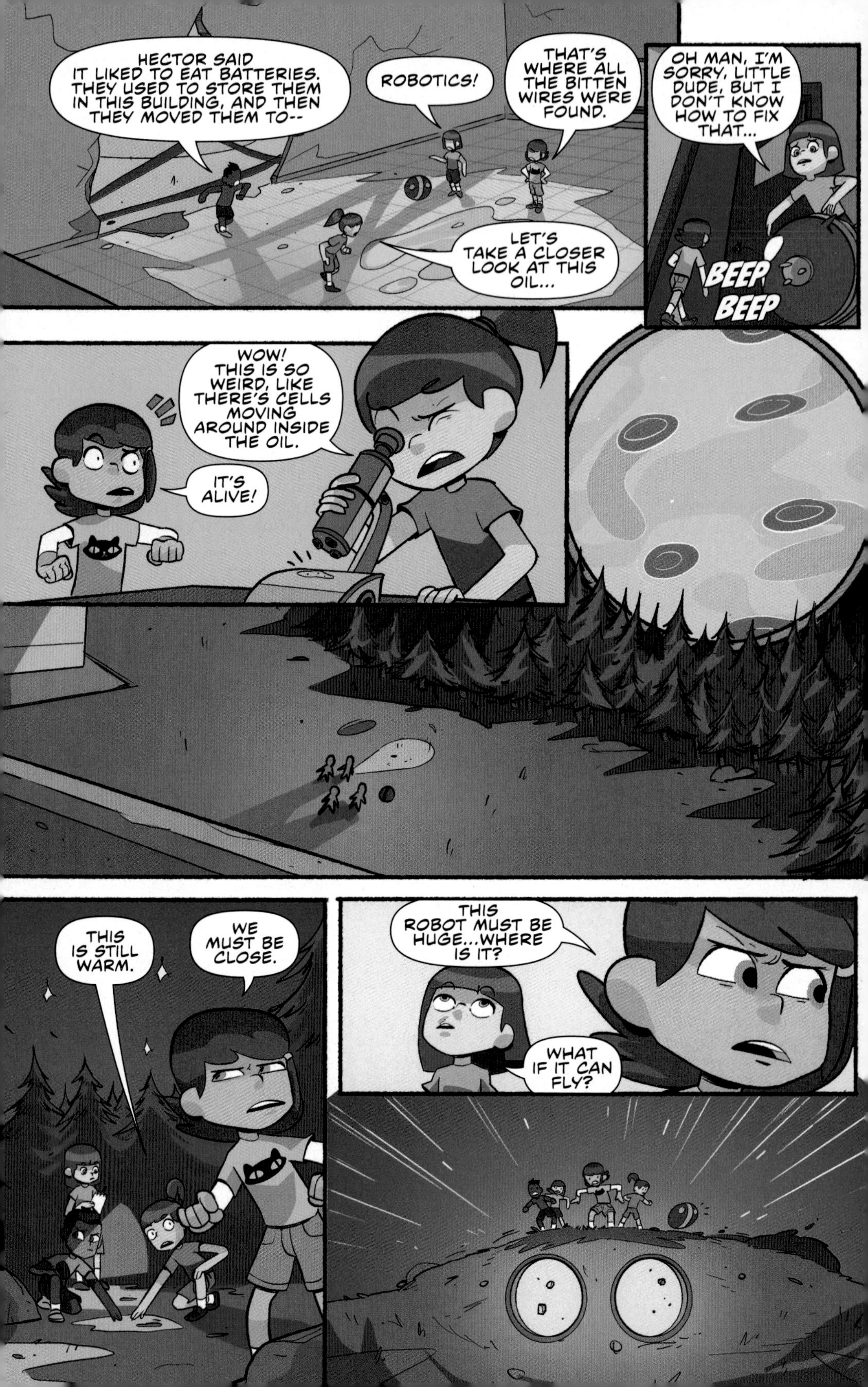
HECTOR SAID IT LIKED TO EAT BATTERIES. THEY USED TO STORE THEM IN THIS BUILDING, AND THEN THEY MOVED THEM TO--
ROBOTICS!
THAT'S WHERE ALL THE BITTEN WIRES WERE FOUND.
LET'S TAKE A CLOSER LOOK AT THIS OIL...
OH MAN, I'M SORRY, LITTLE DUDE, BUT I DON'T KNOW HOW TO FIX THAT...
BEEP
BEEP
WOW! THIS IS SO WEIRD, LIKE THERE'S CELLS MOVING AROUND INSIDE THE OIL.
IT'S ALIVE!
THIS IS STILL WARM.
WE MUST BE CLOSE.
THIS ROBOT MUST BE HUGE...WHERE IS IT?
WHAT IF IT CAN FLY?

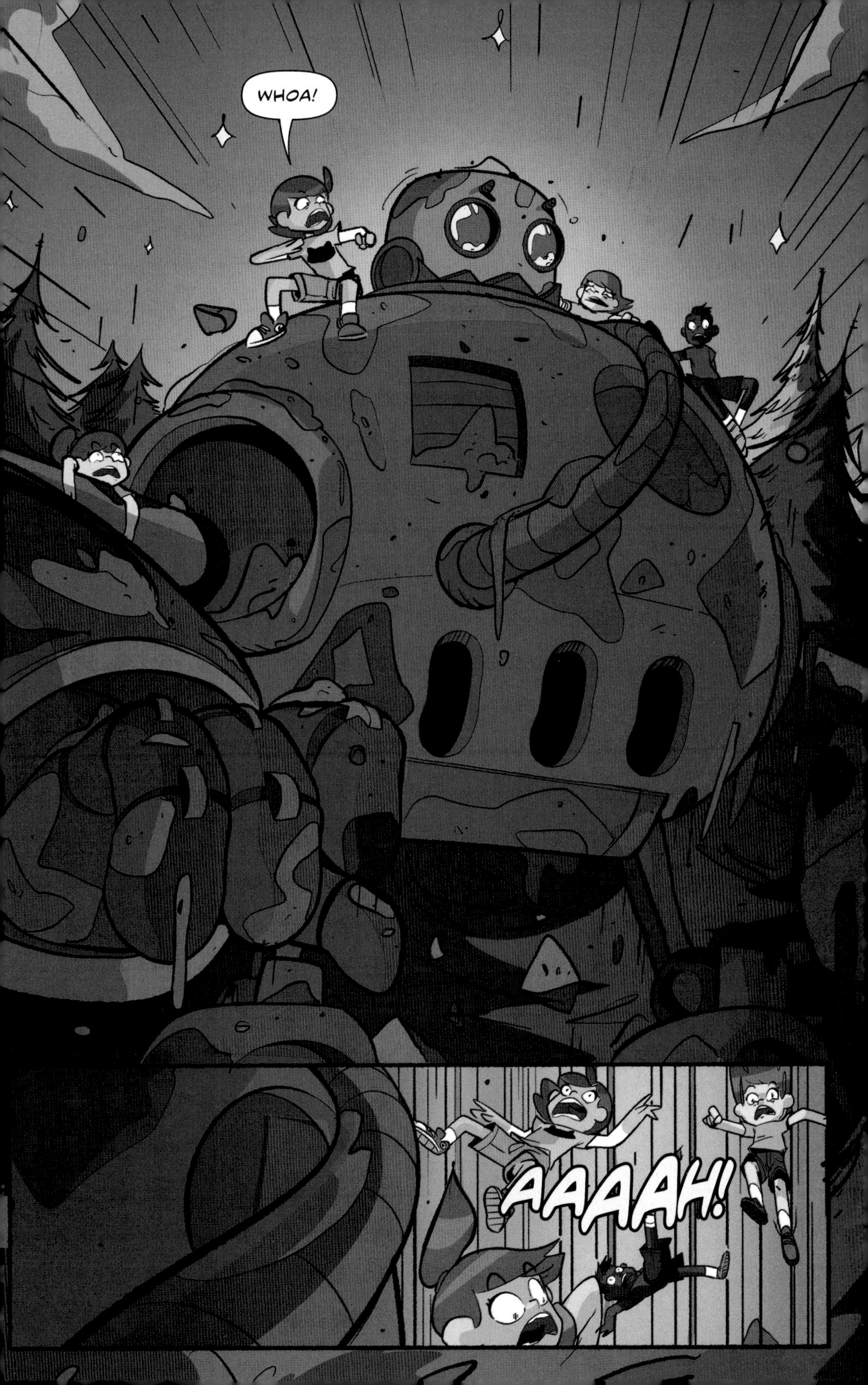
WHOA!
AAAAH!

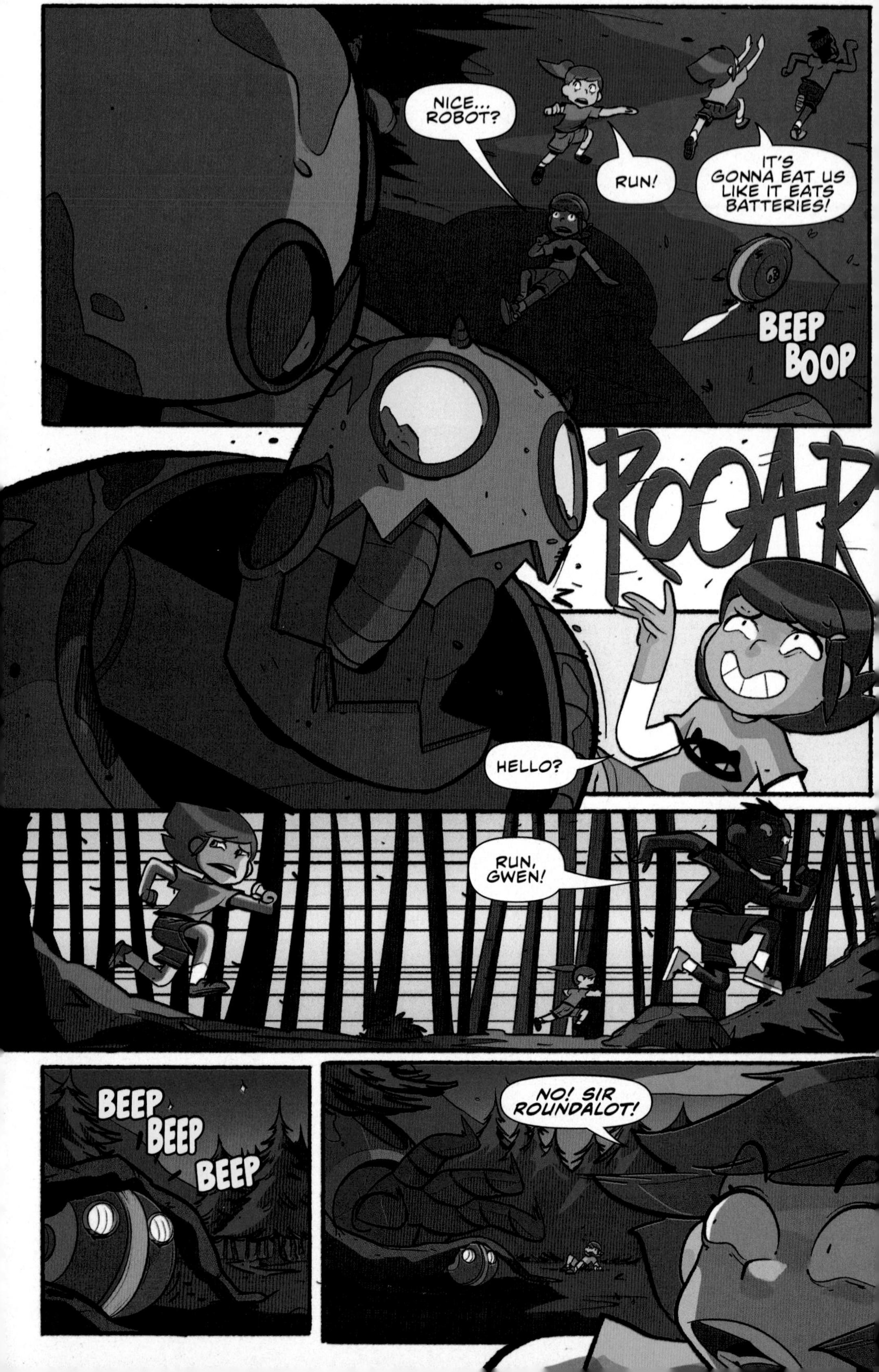
NICE... ROBOT?
RUN!
IT'S GONNA EAT US LIKE IT EATS BATTERIES!
BEEP BOOP
ROOAR
HELLO?
RUN, GWEN!
BEEP BEEP BEEP
NO! SIR ROUNDALOT!

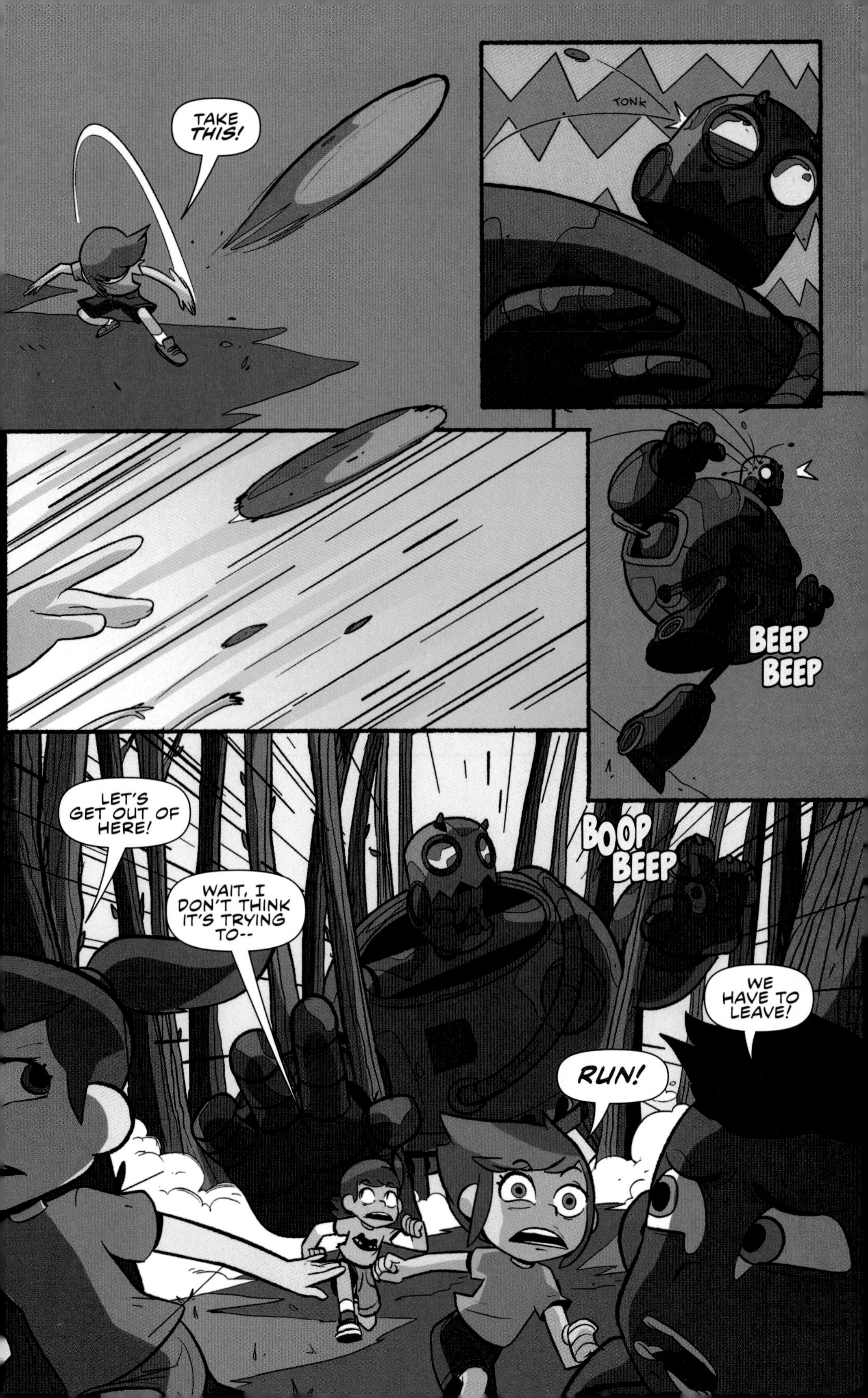
TAKE THIS!
TONK
BEEP BEEP
LET'S GET OUT OF HERE!
WAIT, I DON'T THINK IT'S TRYING TO--
BOOP BEEP
WE HAVE TO LEAVE!
RUN!

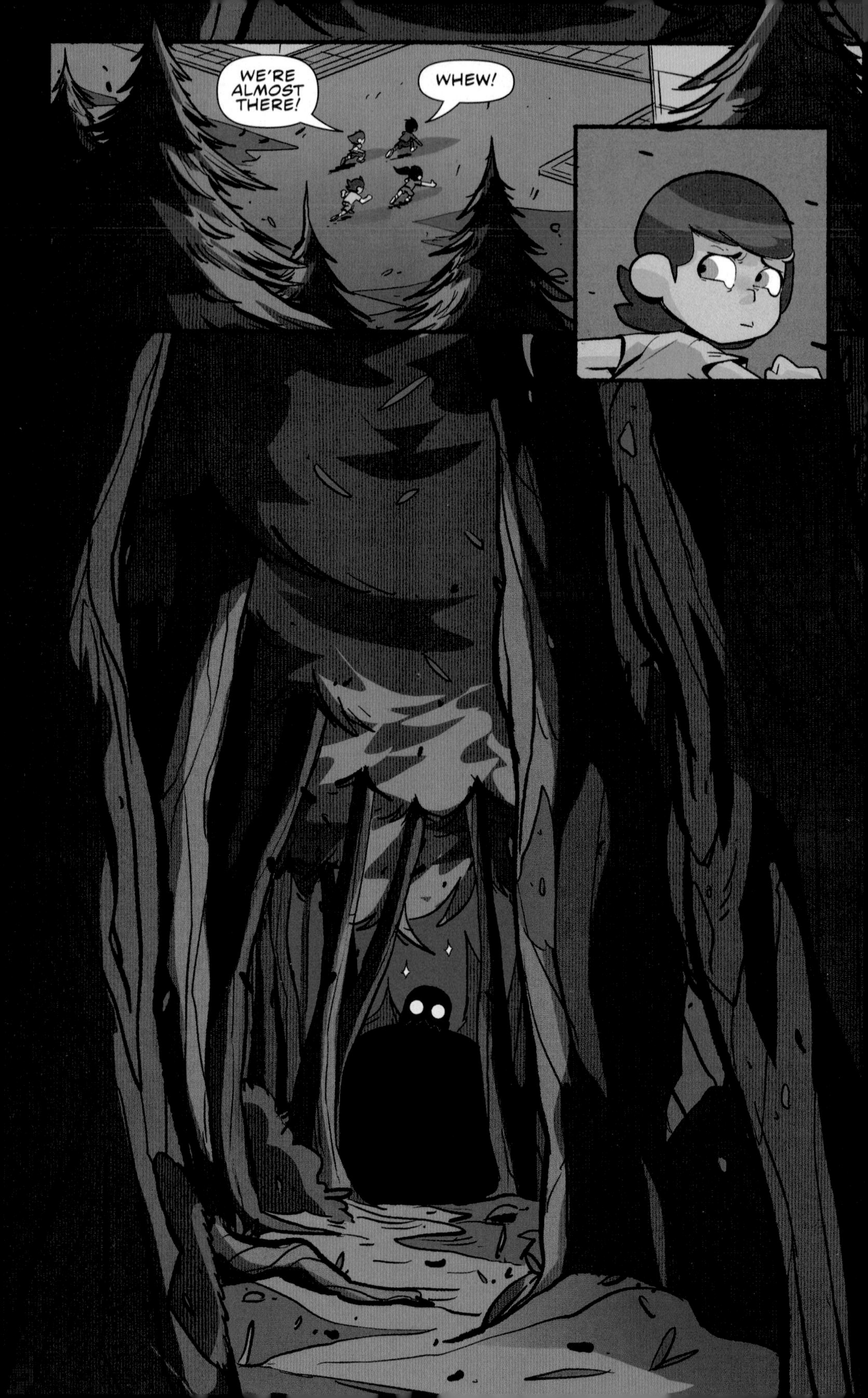
WE'RE ALMOST THERE!
WHEW!

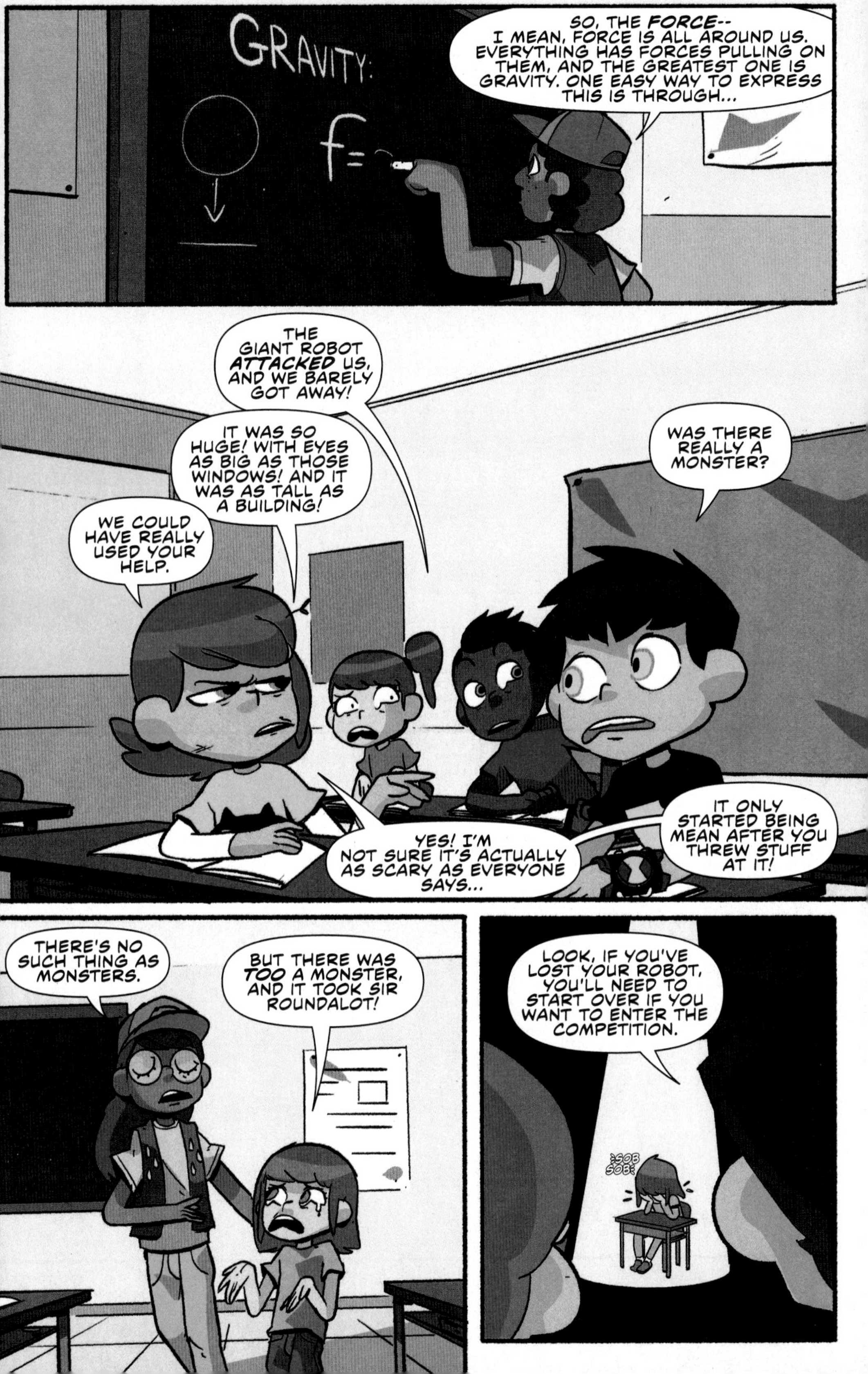
GRAVITY:
f=
SO, THE FORCE-- I MEAN, FORCE IS ALL AROUND US. EVERYTHING HAS FORCES PULLING ON THEM, AND THE GREATEST ONE IS GRAVITY. ONE EASY WAY TO EXPRESS THIS IS THROUGH...
THE GIANT ROBOT ATTACKED US, AND WE BARELY GOT AWAY!
IT WAS SO HUGE! WITH EYES AS BIG AS THOSE WINDOWS! AND IT WAS AS TALL AS A BUILDING!
WE COULD HAVE REALLY USED YOUR HELP.
WAS THERE REALLY A MONSTER?
YES! I'M NOT SURE IT'S ACTUALLY AS SCARY AS EVERYONE SAYS...
IT ONLY STARTED BEING MEAN AFTER YOU THREW STUFF AT IT!
THERE'S NO SUCH THING AS MONSTERS.
BUT THERE WAS TOO A MONSTER, AND IT TOOK SIR ROUNDALOT!
LOOK, IF YOU'VE LOST YOUR ROBOT, YOU'LL NEED TO START OVER IF YOU WANT TO ENTER THE COMPETITION.
SOB SOB

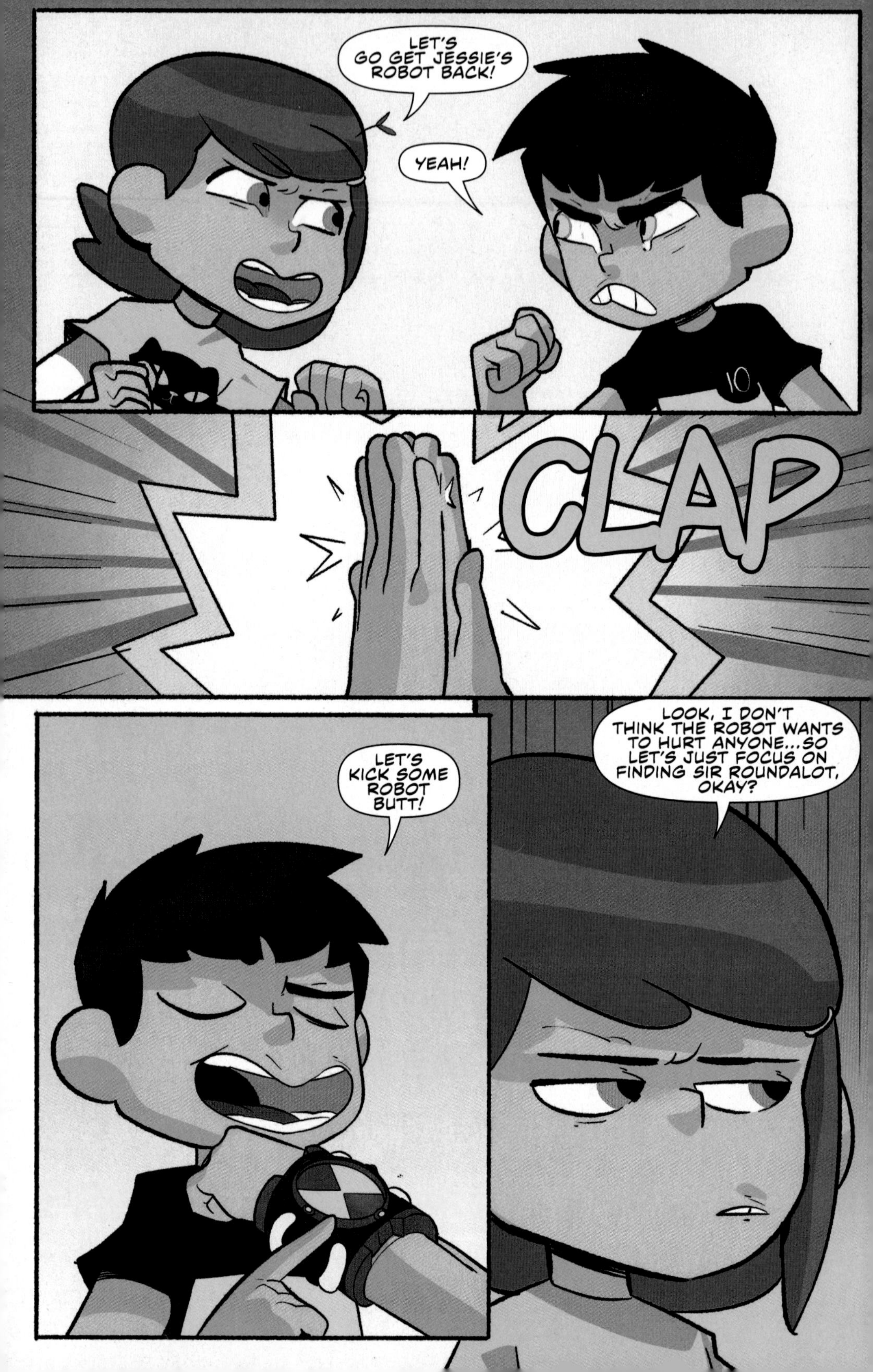
LET'S GO GET JESSIE'S ROBOT BACK!
YEAH!
CLAP
LET'S KICK SOME ROBOT BUTT!
LOOK, I DON'T THINK THE ROBOT WANTS TO HURT ANYONE...SO LET'S JUST FOCUS ON FINDING SIR ROUNDALOT, OKAY?

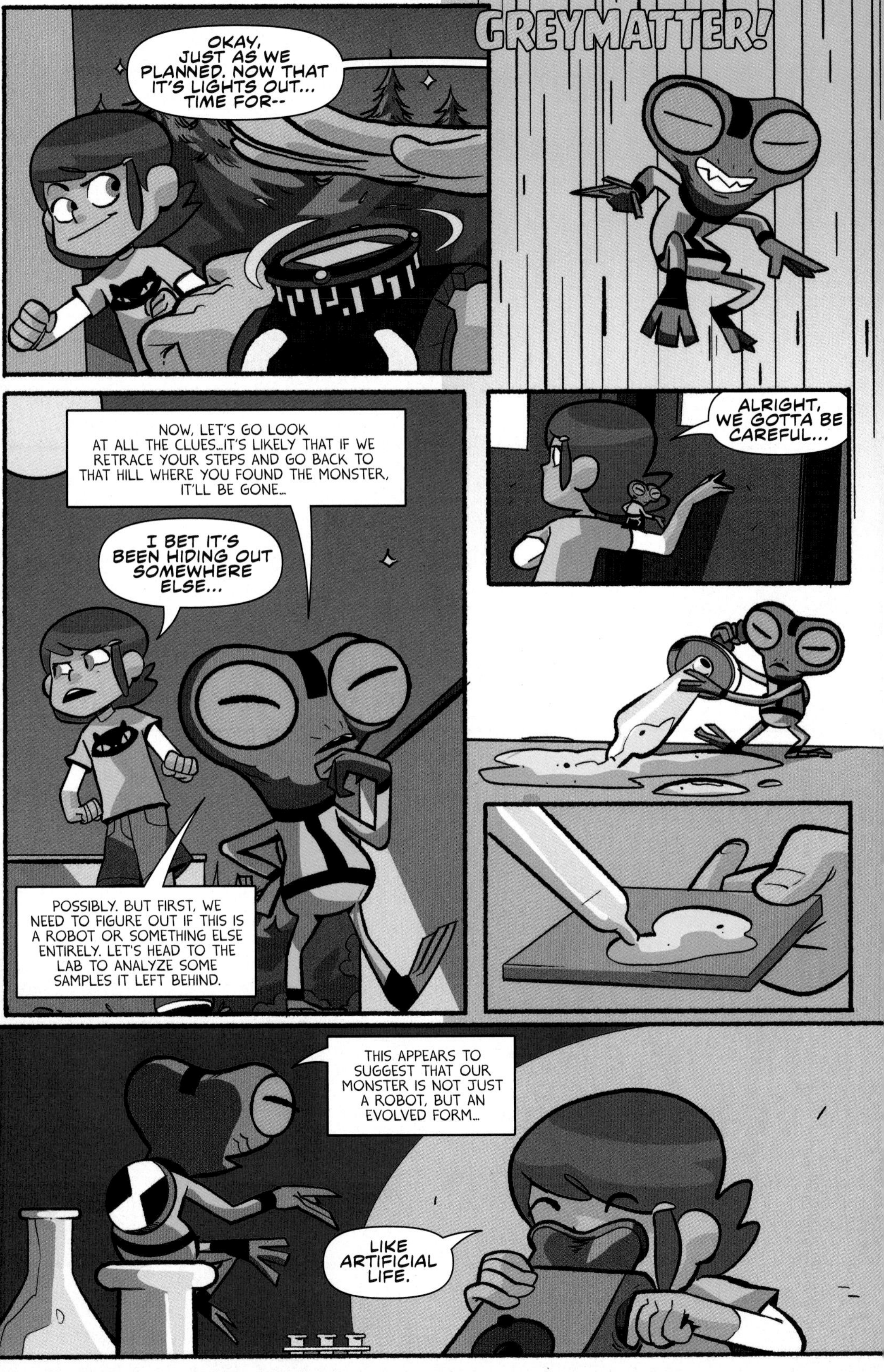
OKAY, JUST AS WE PLANNED. NOW THAT IT'S LIGHTS OUT... TIME FOR--
GREYMATTER!
NOW, LET'S GO LOOK AT ALL THE CLUES...IT'S LIKELY THAT IF WE RETRACE YOUR STEPS AND GO BACK TO THAT HILL WHERE YOU FOUND THE MONSTER, IT'LL BE GONE...
I BET IT'S BEEN HIDING OUT SOMEWHERE ELSE...
POSSIBLY. BUT FIRST, WE NEED TO FIGURE OUT IF THIS IS A ROBOT OR SOMETHING ELSE ENTIRELY. LET'S HEAD TO THE LAB TO ANALYZE SOME SAMPLES IT LEFT BEHIND.
ALRIGHT, WE GOTTA BE CAREFUL...
THIS APPEARS TO SUGGEST THAT OUR MONSTER IS NOT JUST A ROBOT, BUT AN EVOLVED FORM...
LIKE ARTIFICIAL LIFE.

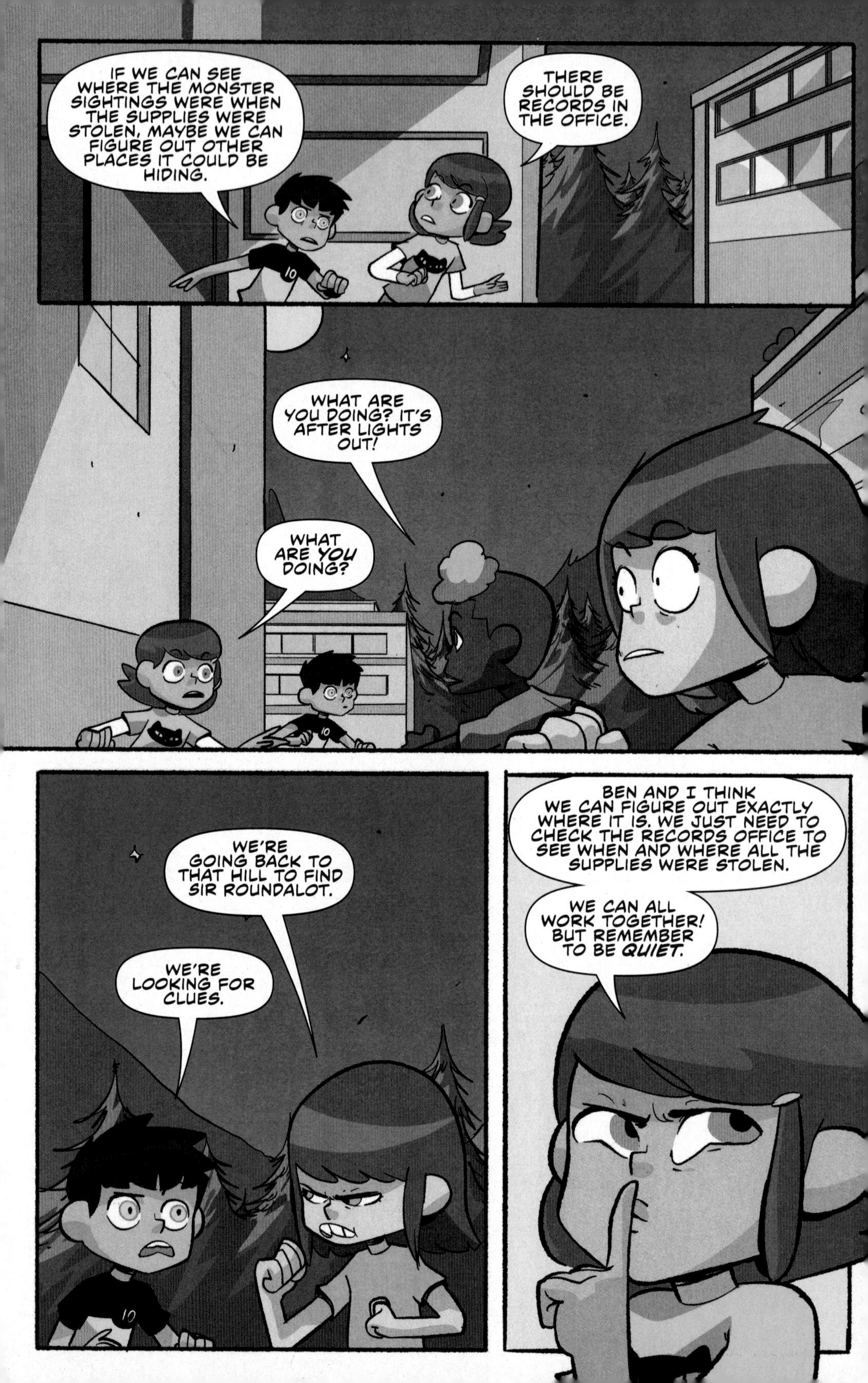
IF WE CAN SEE WHERE THE MONSTER SIGHTINGS WERE WHEN THE SUPPLIES WERE STOLEN, MAYBE WE CAN FIGURE OUT OTHER PLACES IT COULD BE HIDING.
THERE SHOULD BE RECORDS IN THE OFFICE.
WHAT ARE YOU DOING? IT'S AFTER LIGHTS OUT!
WHAT ARE *YOU* DOING?
WE'RE GOING BACK TO THAT HILL TO FIND SIR ROUNDALOT.
WE'RE LOOKING FOR CLUES.
BEN AND I THINK WE CAN FIGURE OUT EXACTLY WHERE IT IS. WE JUST NEED TO CHECK THE RECORDS OFFICE TO SEE WHEN AND WHERE ALL THE SUPPLIES WERE STOLEN.
WE CAN ALL WORK TOGETHER! BUT REMEMBER TO BE *QUIET*.

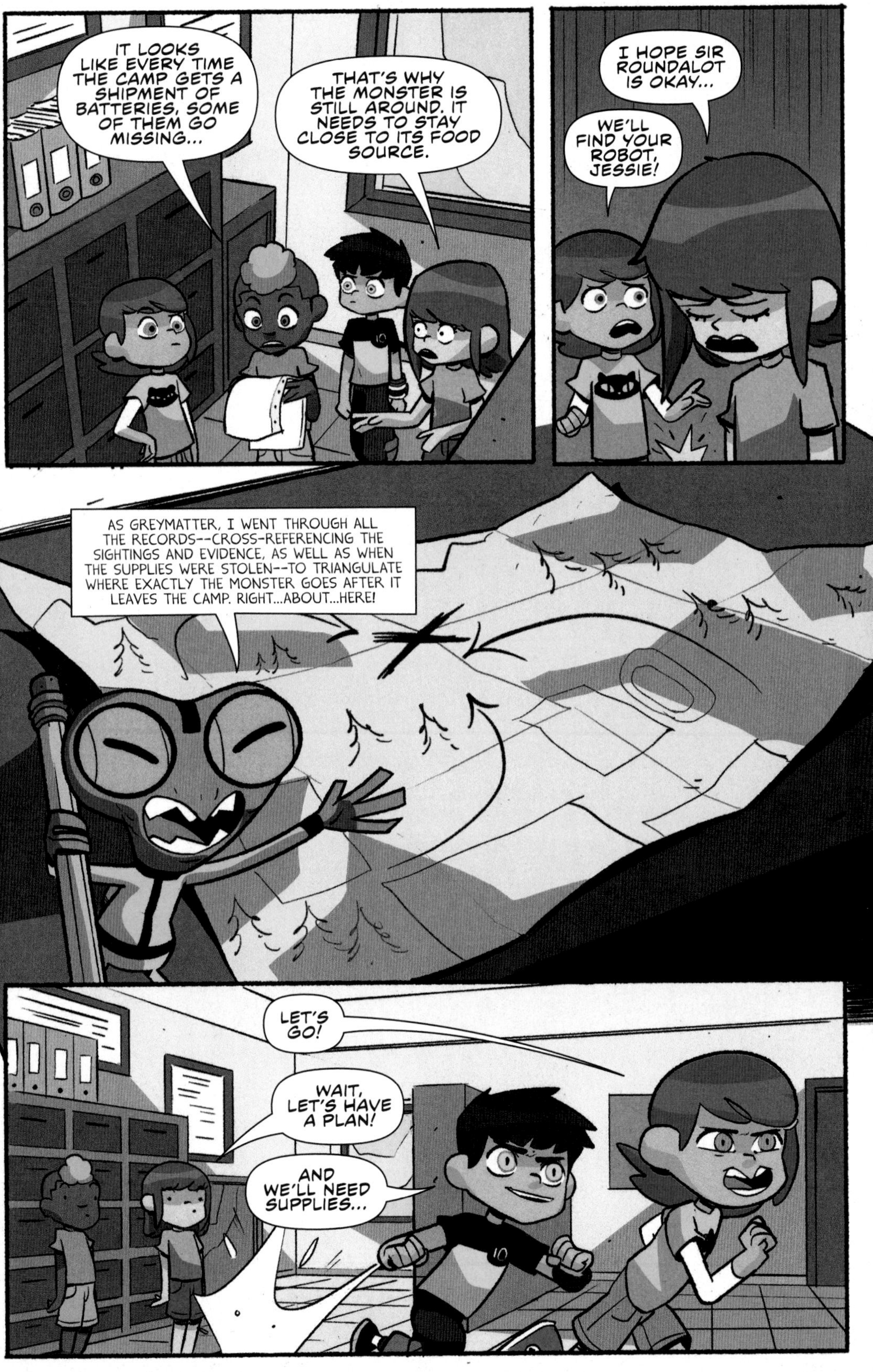
IT LOOKS LIKE EVERY TIME THE CAMP GETS A SHIPMENT OF BATTERIES, SOME OF THEM GO MISSING...
THAT'S WHY THE MONSTER IS STILL AROUND. IT NEEDS TO STAY CLOSE TO ITS FOOD SOURCE.
I HOPE SIR ROUNDALOT IS OKAY...
WE'LL FIND YOUR ROBOT, JESSIE!
AS GREYMATTER, I WENT THROUGH ALL THE RECORDS--CROSS-REFERENCING THE SIGHTINGS AND EVIDENCE, AS WELL AS WHEN THE SUPPLIES WERE STOLEN--TO TRIANGULATE WHERE EXACTLY THE MONSTER GOES AFTER IT LEAVES THE CAMP. RIGHT...ABOUT...HERE!
LET'S GO!
WAIT, LET'S HAVE A PLAN!
AND WE'LL NEED SUPPLIES...

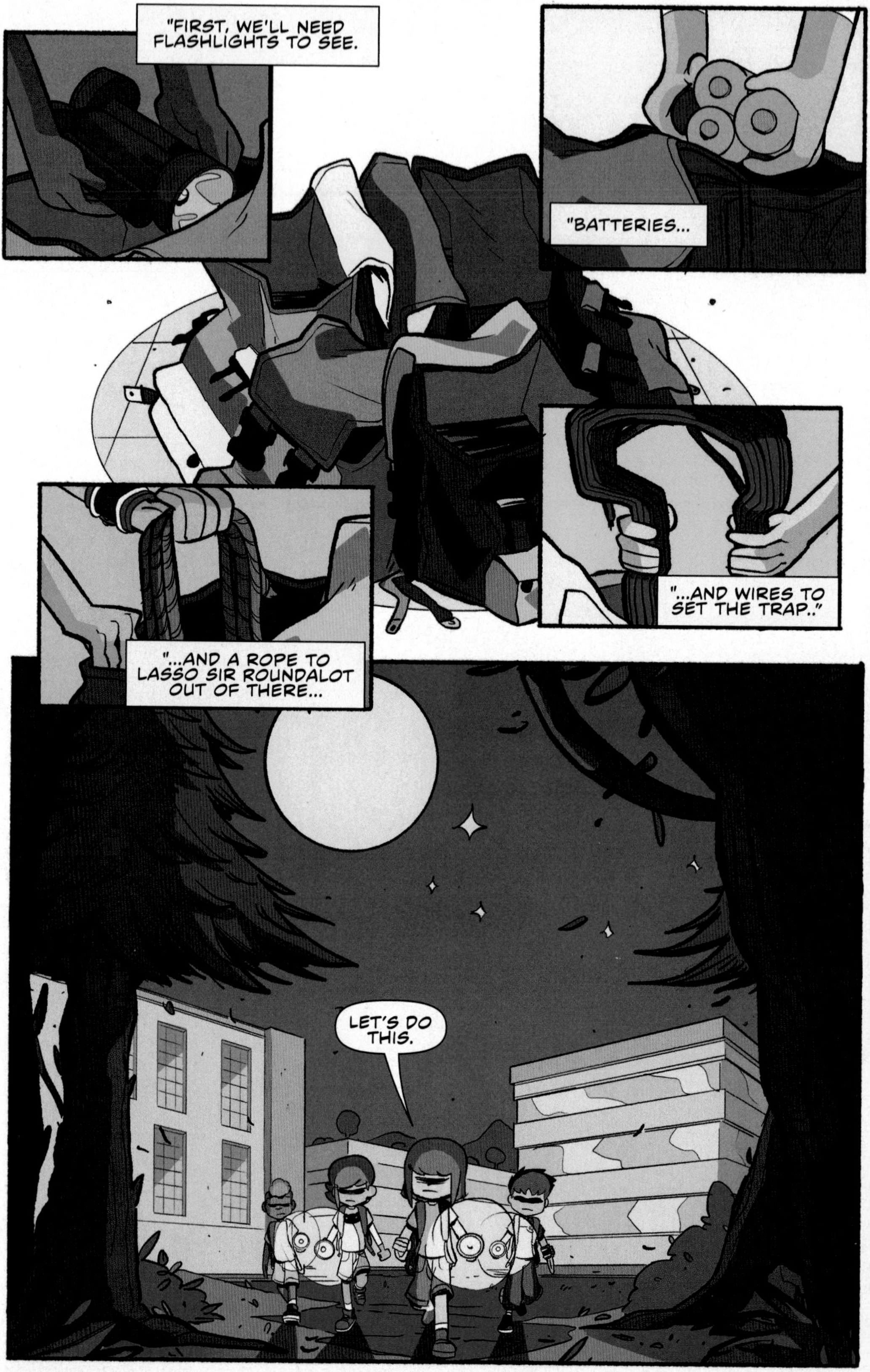
"FIRST, WE'LL NEED FLASHLIGHTS TO SEE.
"BATTERIES...
"...AND WIRES TO SET THE TRAP.."
"...AND A ROPE TO LASSO SIR ROUNDALOT OUT OF THERE...
LET'S DO THIS.

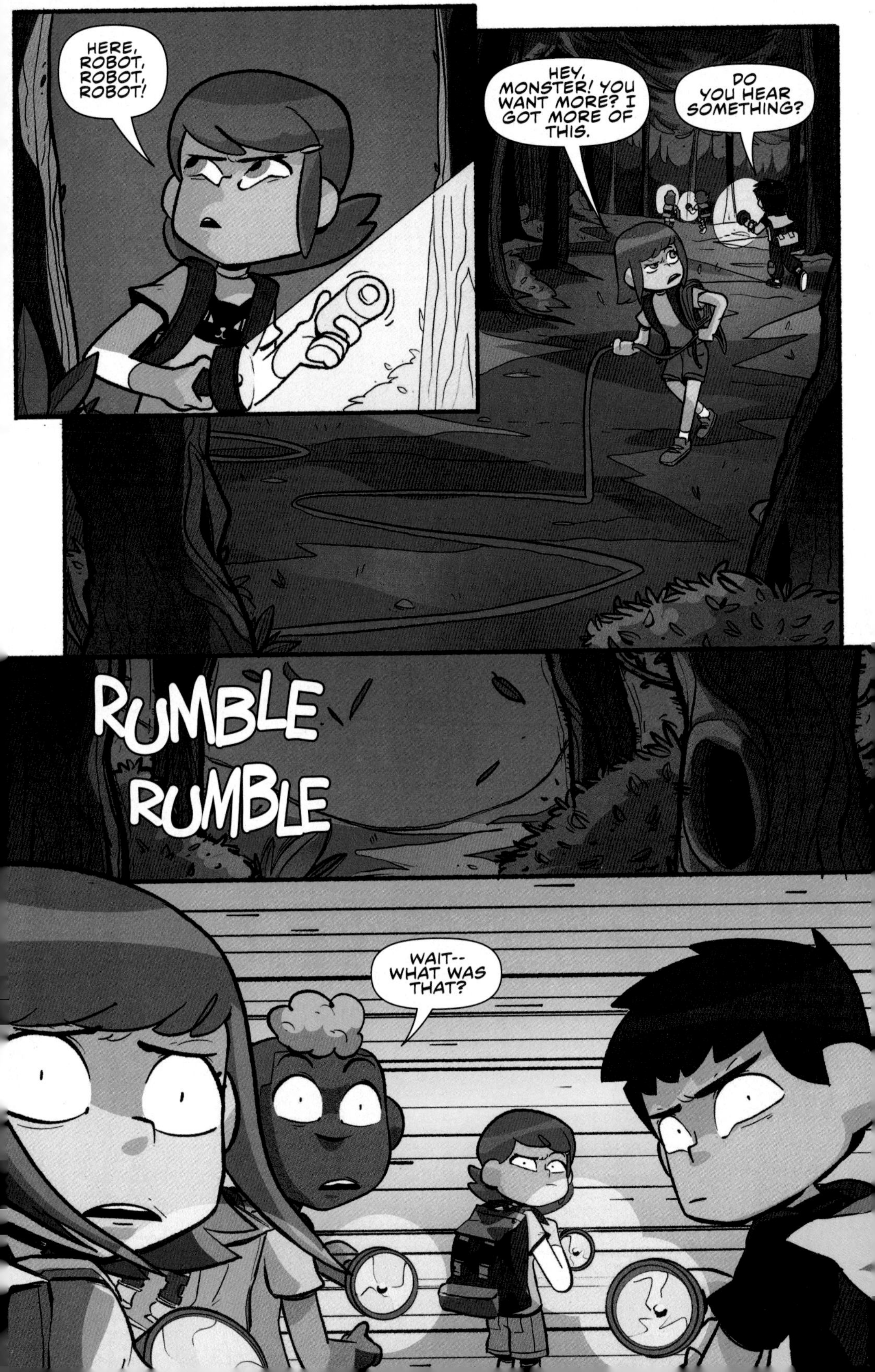
HERE, ROBOT, ROBOT, ROBOT!
HEY, MONSTER! YOU WANT MORE? I GOT MORE OF THIS.
DO YOU HEAR SOMETHING?
RUMBLE
RUMBLE
WAIT-- WHAT WAS THAT?

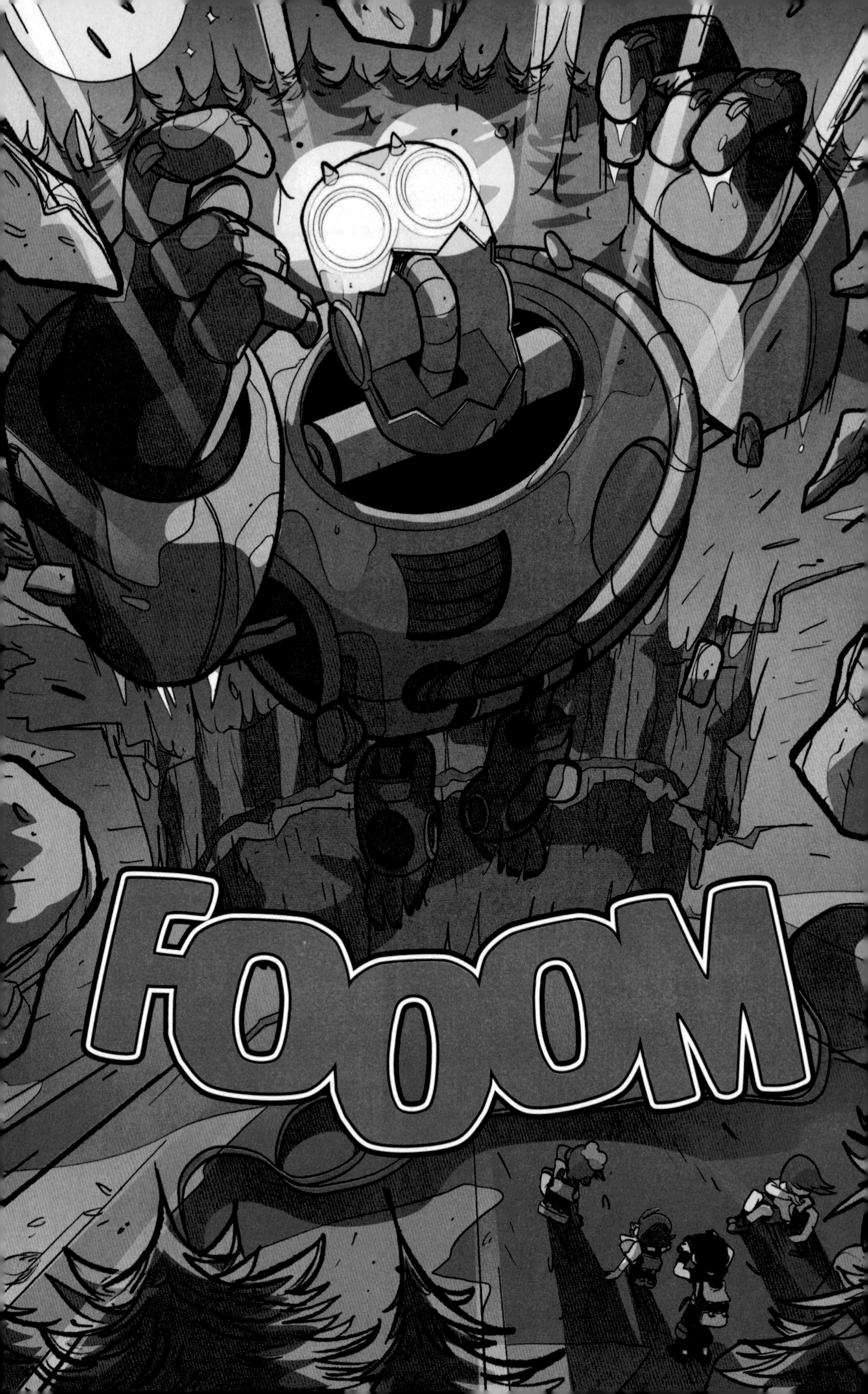
FOOOM

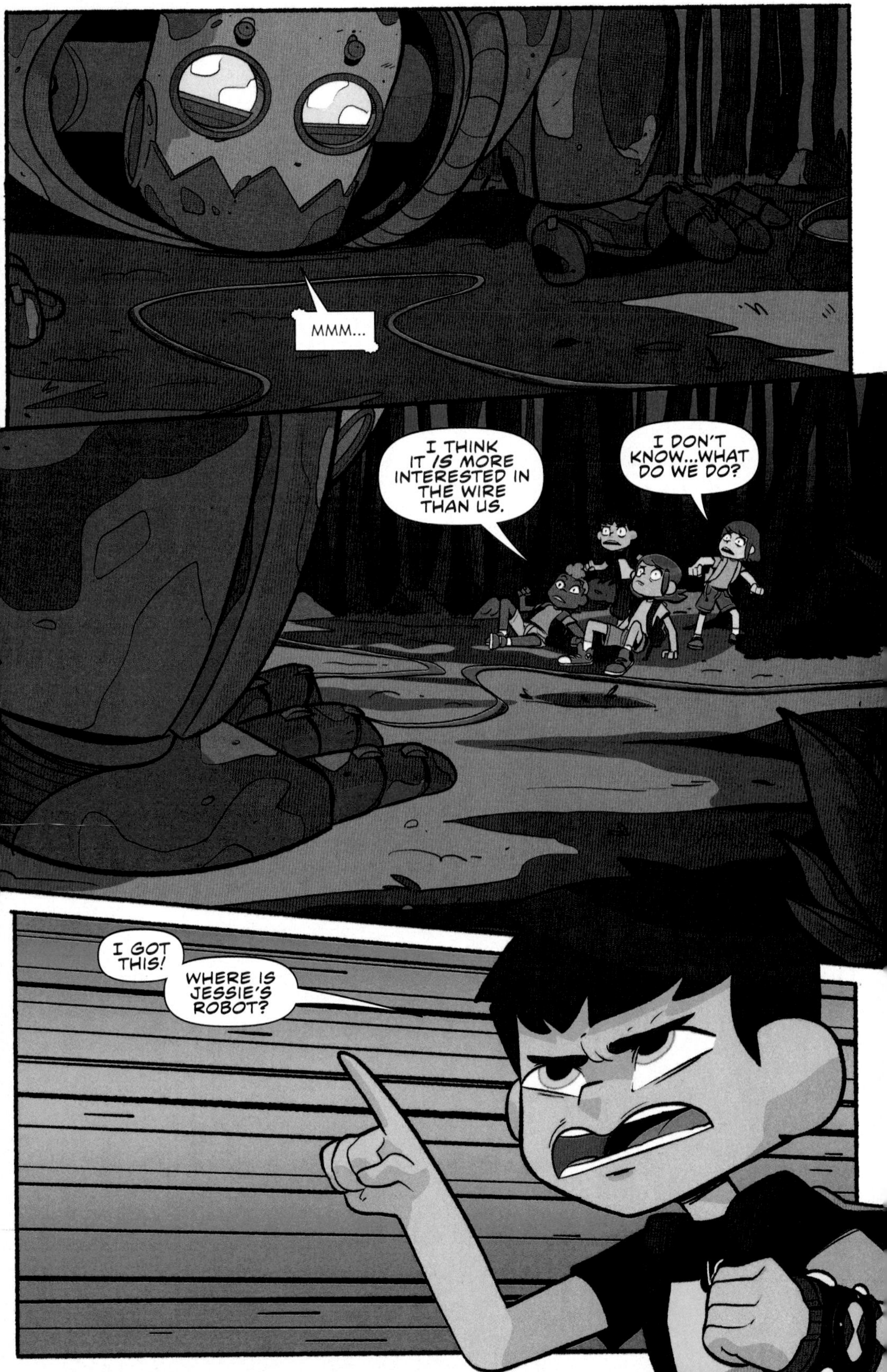
MMM...
I THINK IT *IS* MORE INTERESTED IN THE WIRE THAN US.
I DON'T KNOW...WHAT DO WE DO?
I GOT THIS!
WHERE IS JESSIE'S ROBOT?

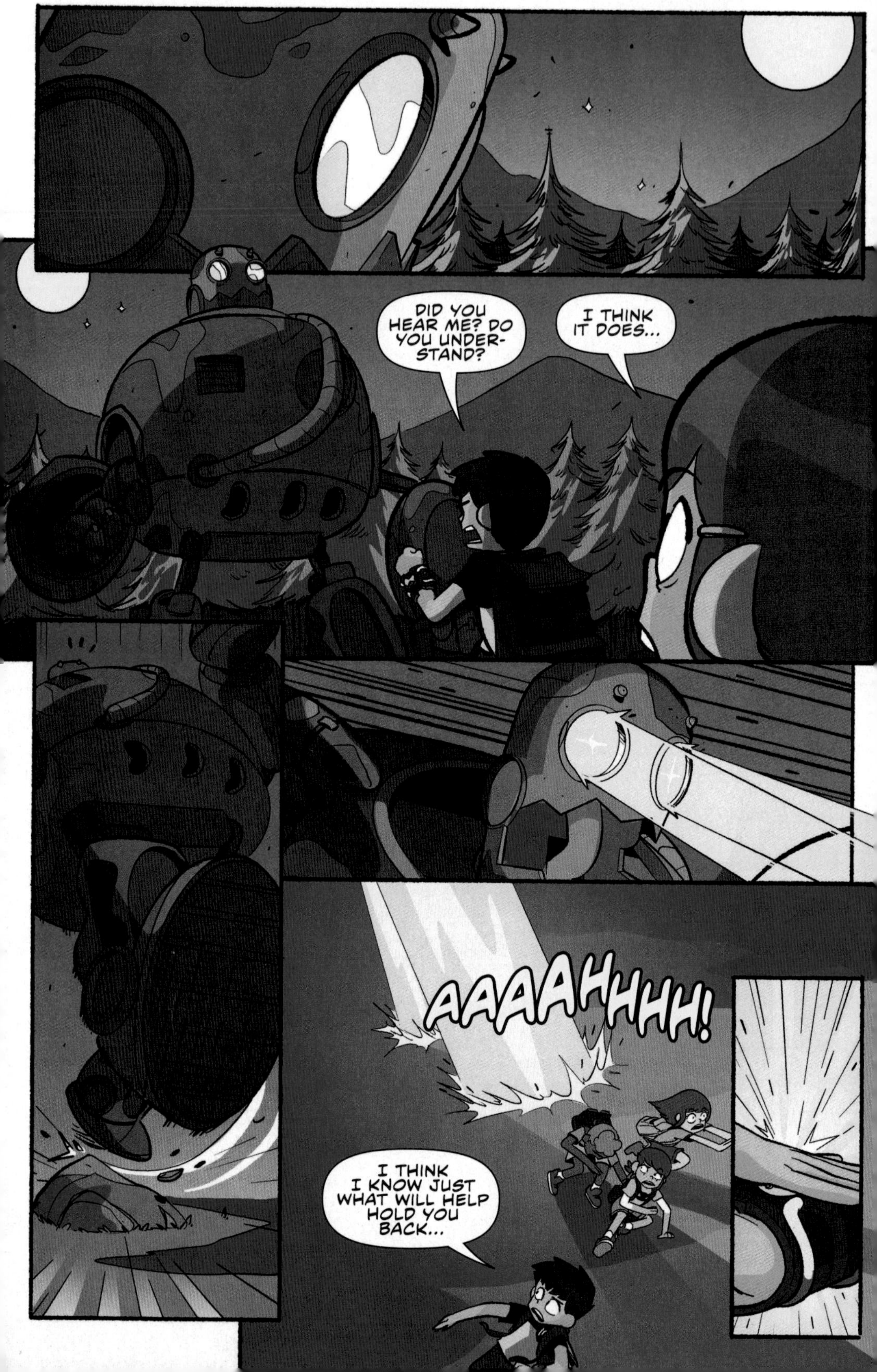
DID YOU HEAR ME? DO YOU UNDER-STAND?
I THINK IT DOES...
AAAAHHHH!
I THINK I KNOW JUST WHAT WILL HELP HOLD YOU BACK...

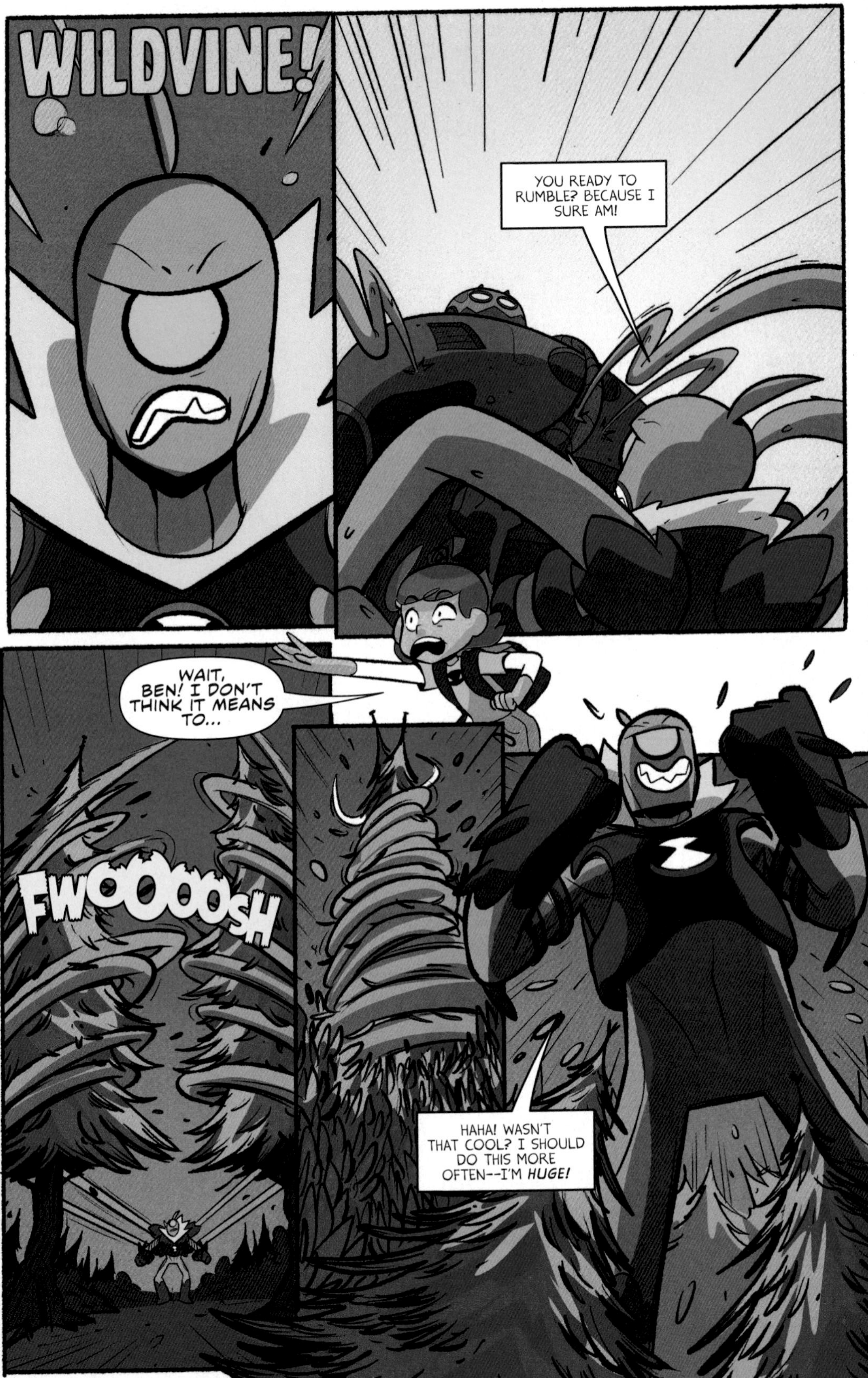
WILDVINE!
YOU READY TO RUMBLE? BECAUSE I SURE AM!
WAIT, BEN! I DON'T THINK IT MEANS TO...
FWOOOOSH
HAHA! WASN'T THAT COOL? I SHOULD DO THIS MORE OFTEN--I'M *HUGE!*

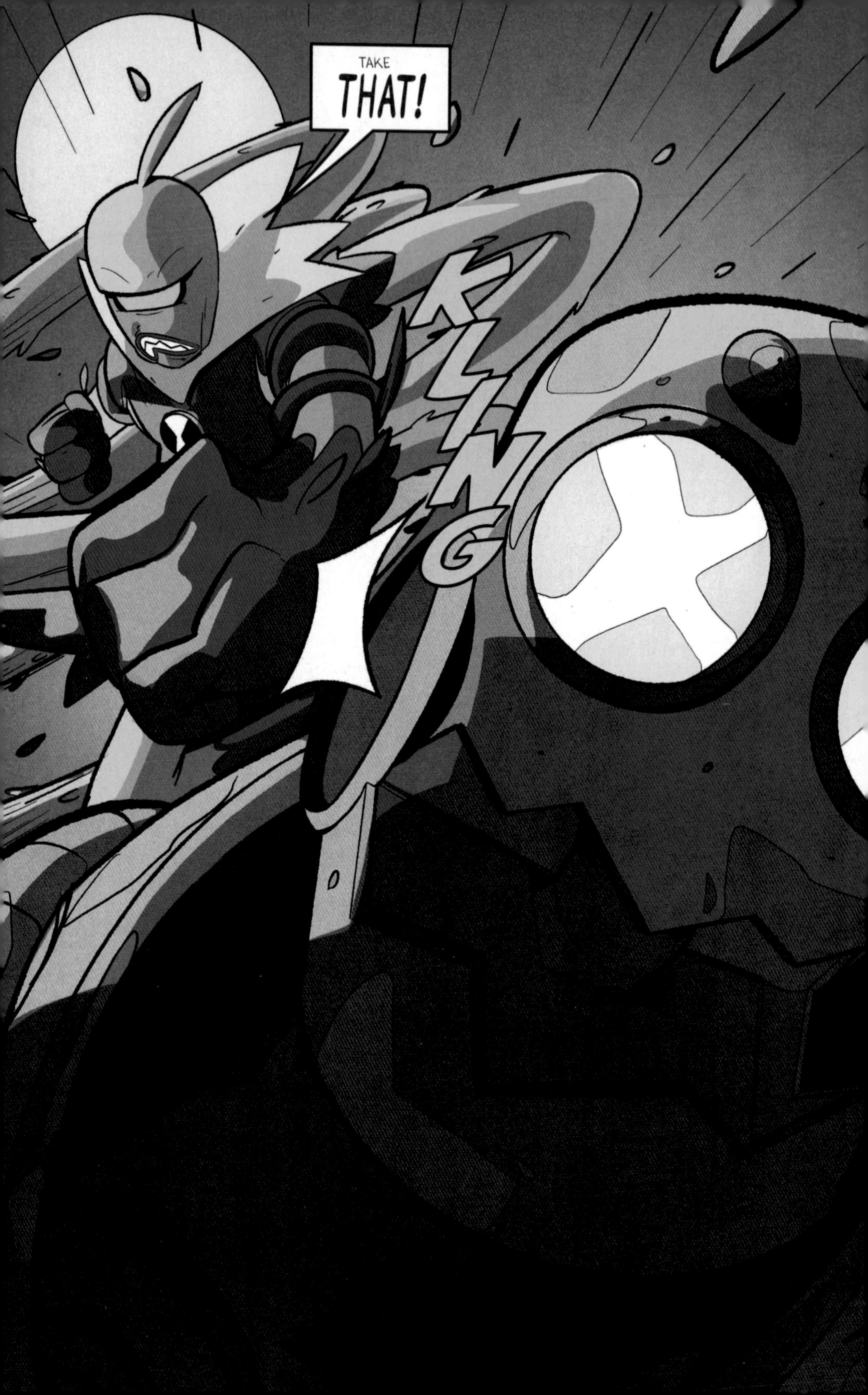
TAKE THAT!
KLING

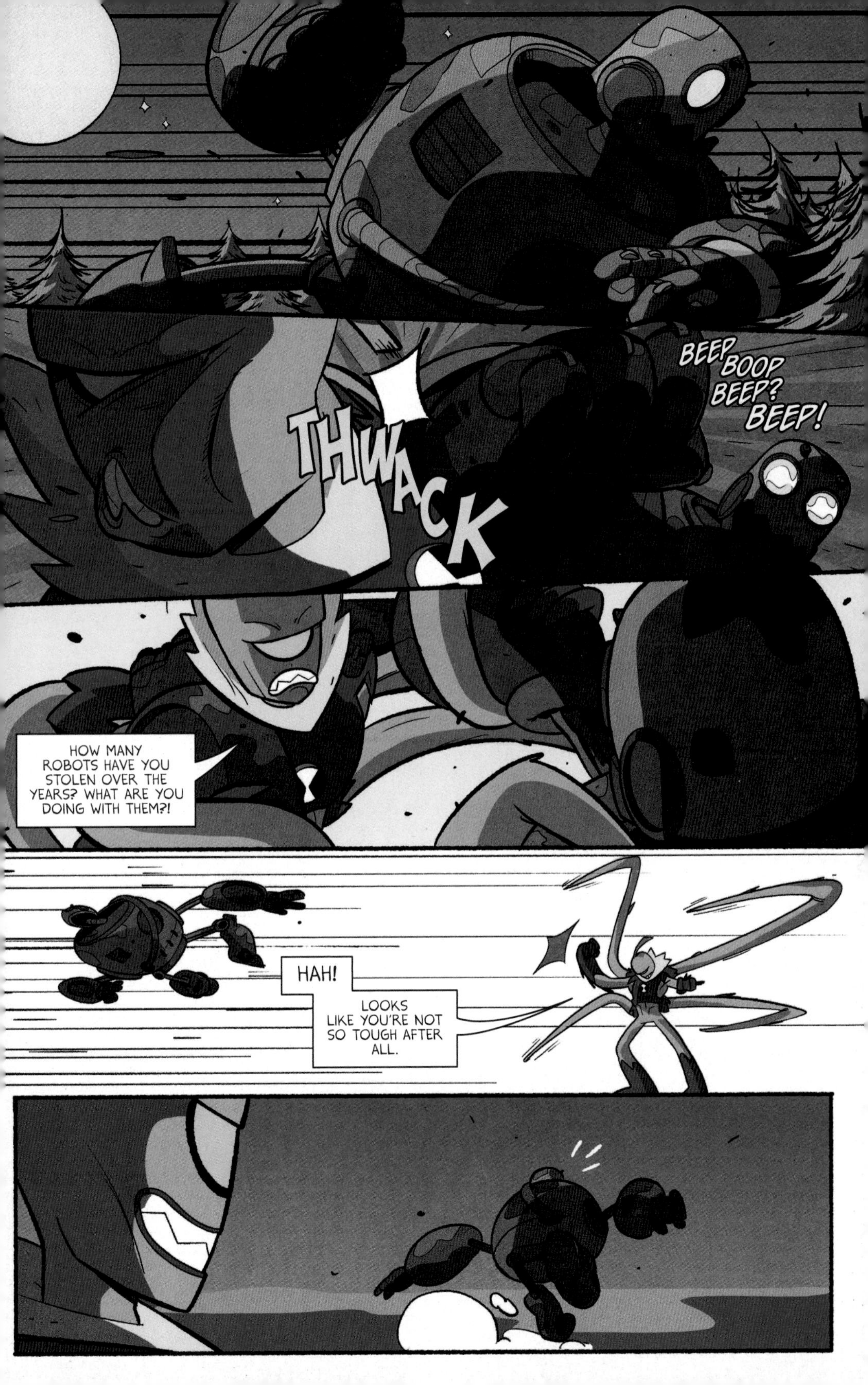
THWACK
BEEP BOOP BEEP? BEEP!
HOW MANY ROBOTS HAVE YOU STOLEN OVER THE YEARS? WHAT ARE YOU DOING WITH THEM?!
HAH!
LOOKS LIKE YOU'RE NOT SO TOUGH AFTER ALL.

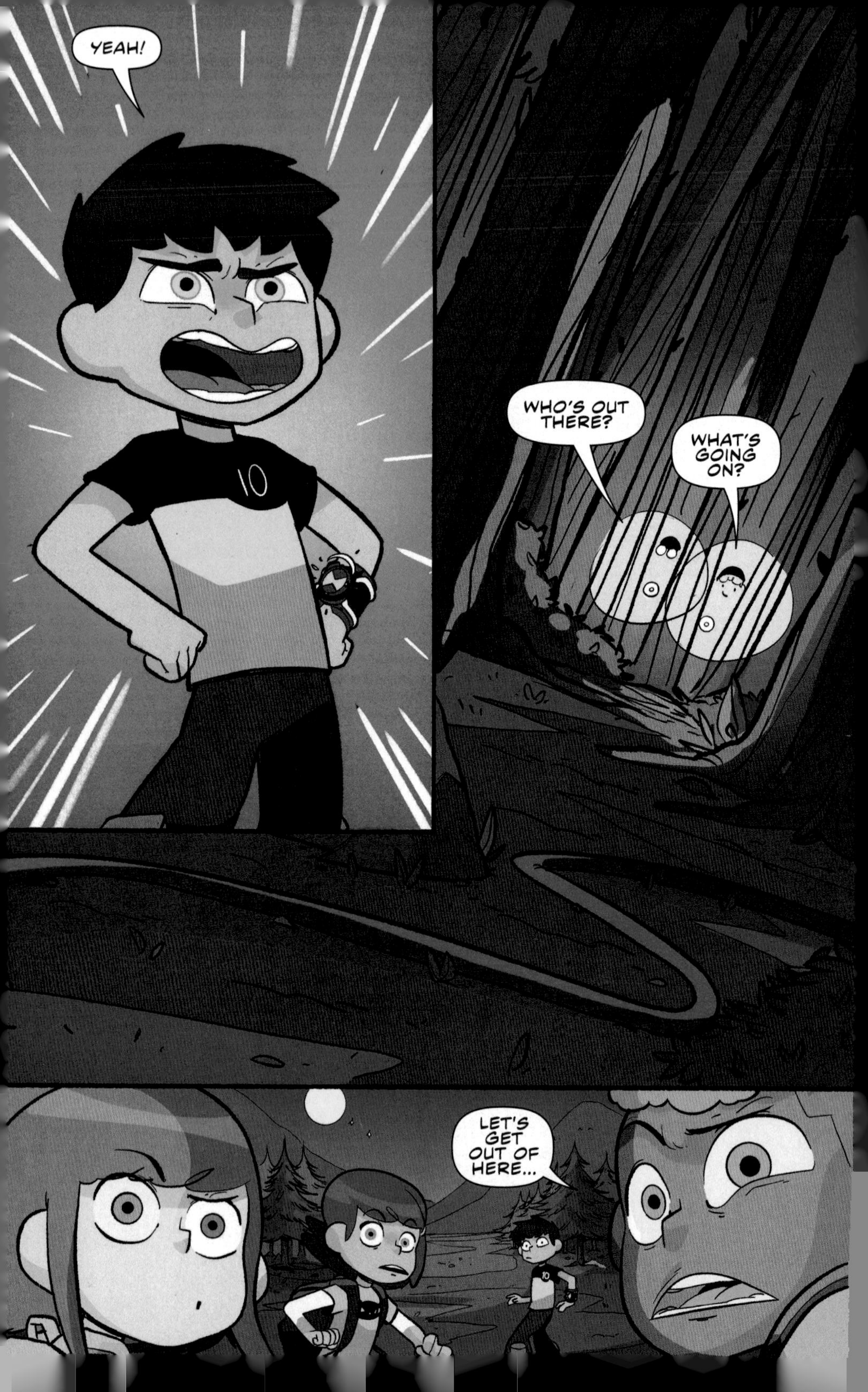
YEAH!
WHO'S OUT THERE?
WHAT'S GOING ON?
LET'S GET OUT OF HERE...

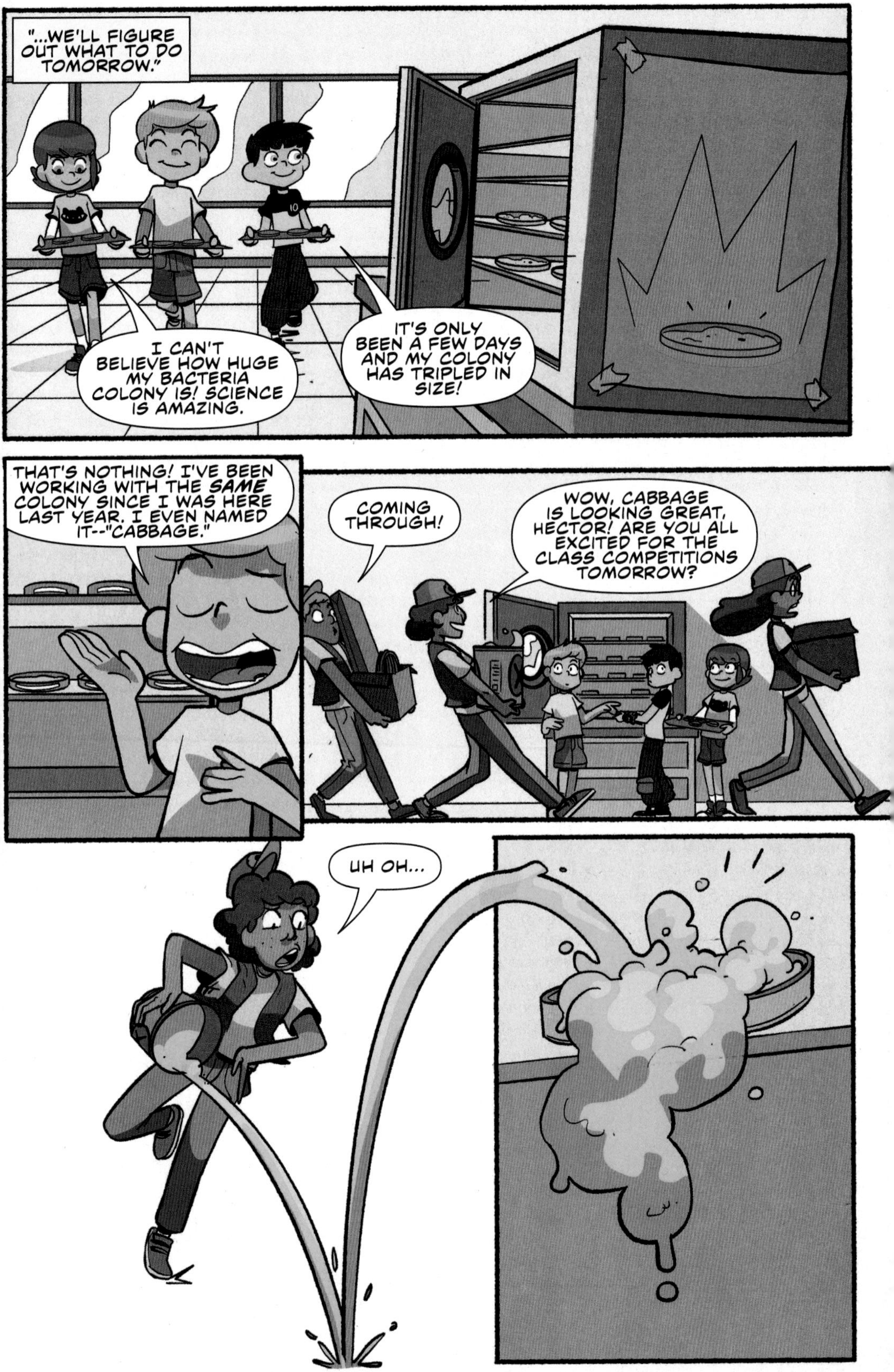
"...WE'LL FIGURE OUT WHAT TO DO TOMORROW."
I CAN'T BELIEVE HOW HUGE MY BACTERIA COLONY IS! SCIENCE IS AMAZING.
IT'S ONLY BEEN A FEW DAYS AND MY COLONY HAS TRIPLED IN SIZE!
THAT'S NOTHING! I'VE BEEN WORKING WITH THE *SAME* COLONY SINCE I WAS HERE LAST YEAR. I EVEN NAMED IT--"CABBAGE."
COMING THROUGH!
WOW, CABBAGE IS LOOKING GREAT, HECTOR! ARE YOU ALL EXCITED FOR THE CLASS COMPETITIONS TOMORROW?
UH OH...

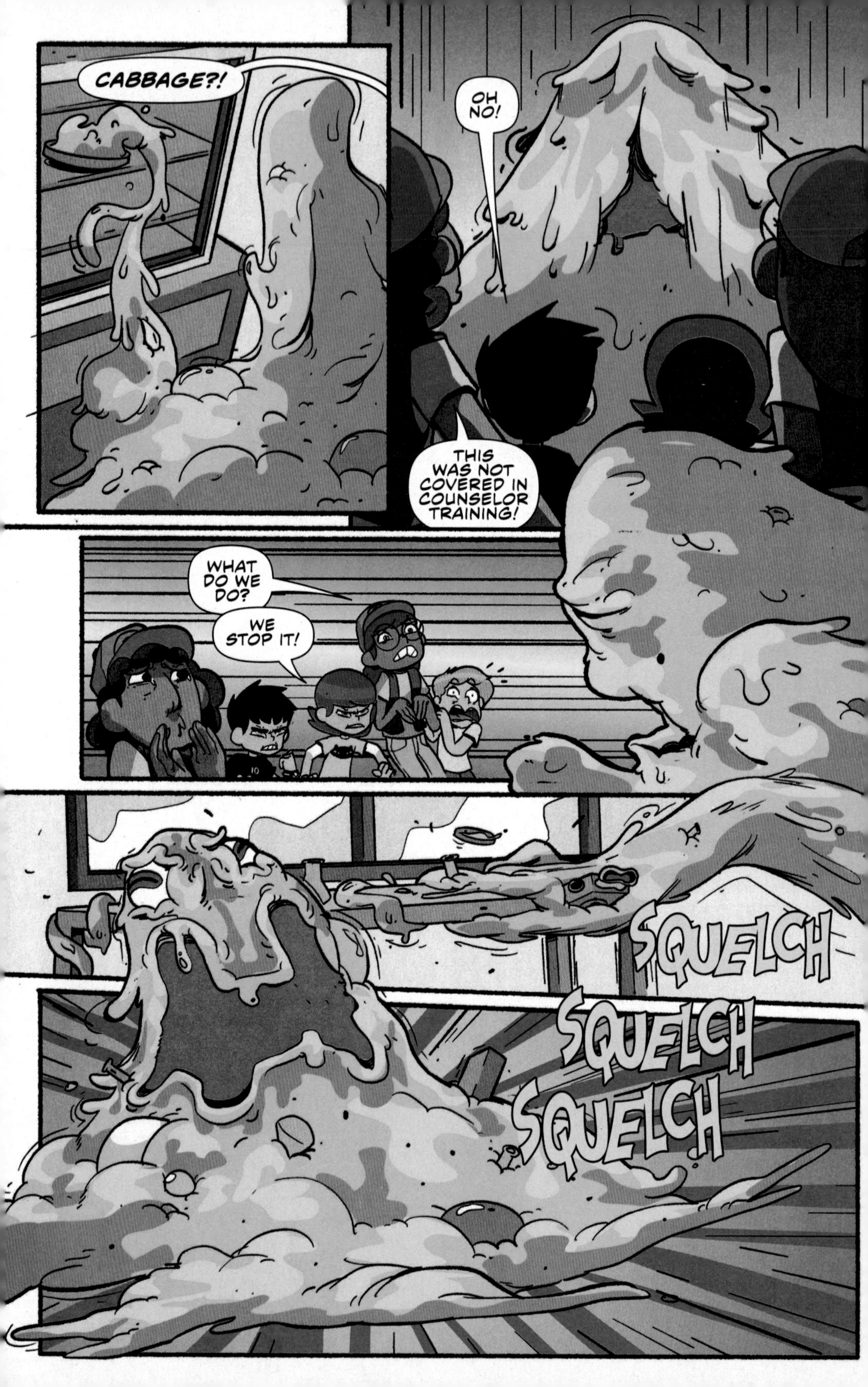
CABBAGE?!
OH NO!
THIS WAS NOT COVERED IN COUNSELOR TRAINING!
WHAT DO WE DO?
WE STOP IT!
SQUELCH
SQUELCH
SQUELCH

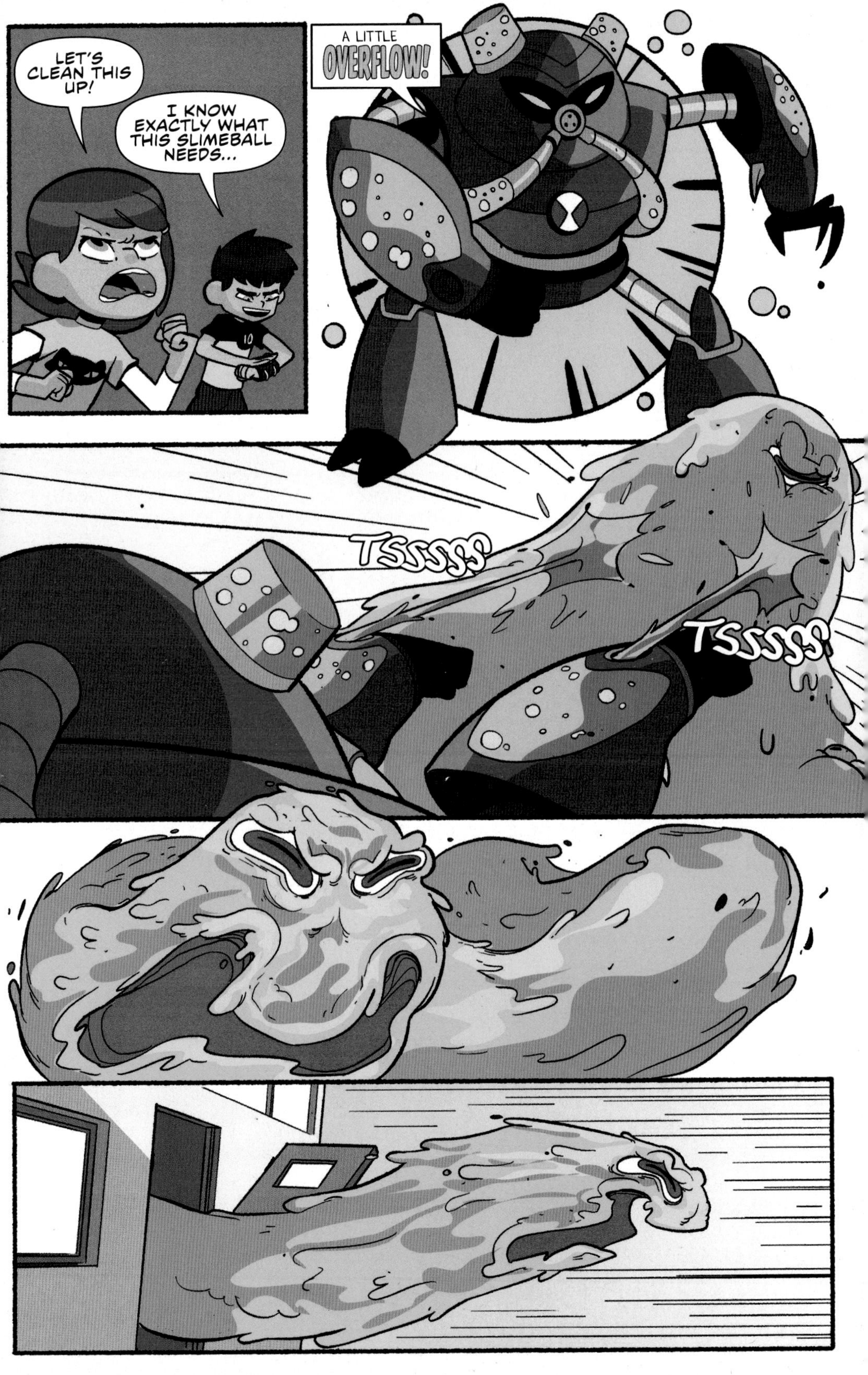

LET'S CLEAN THIS UP!
I KNOW EXACTLY WHAT THIS SLIMEBALL NEEDS...
A LITTLE OVERFLOW!
TSSSSS
TSSSSS

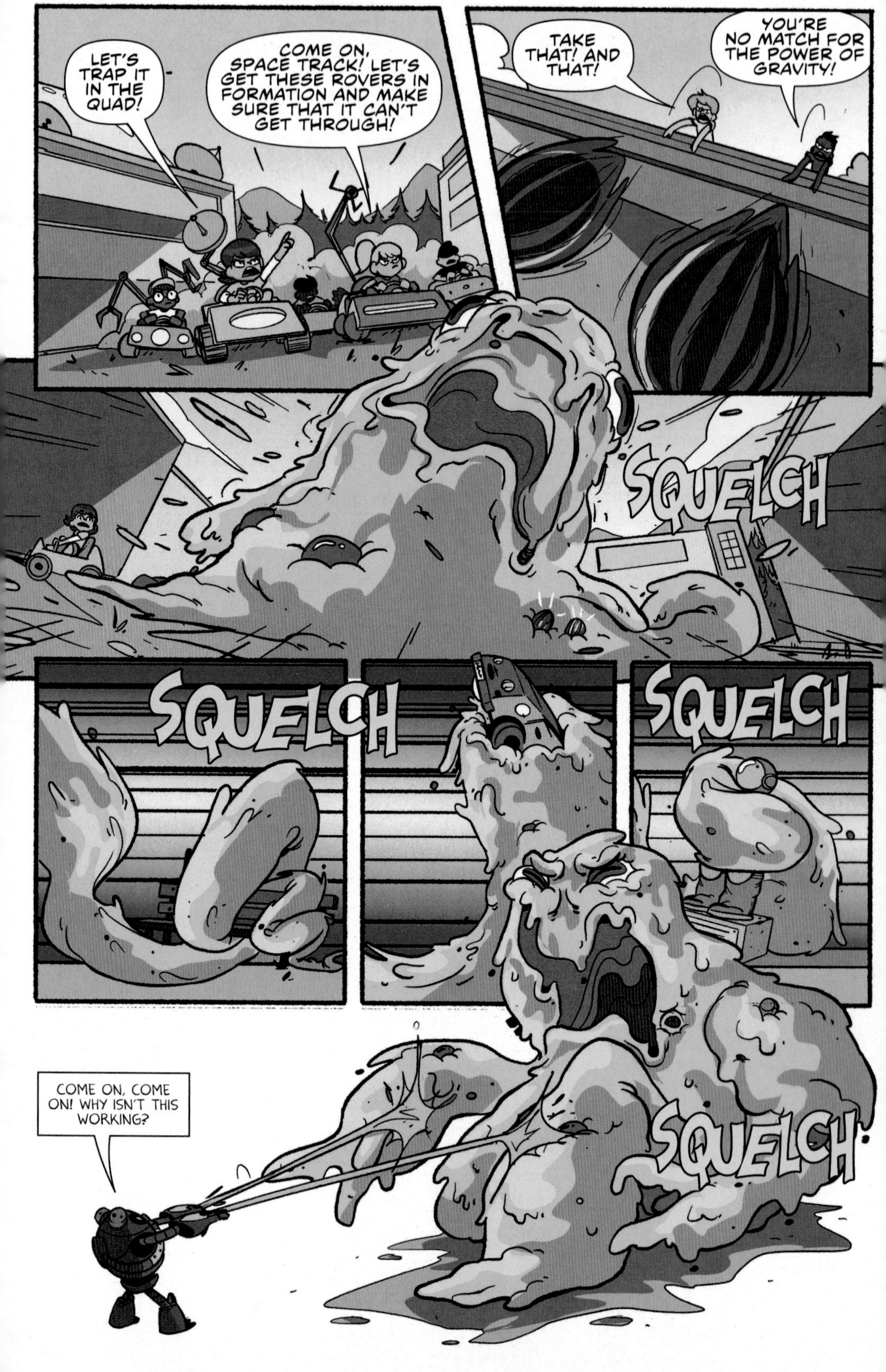
LET'S TRAP IT IN THE QUAD!
COME ON, SPACE TRACK! LET'S GET THESE ROVERS IN FORMATION AND MAKE SURE THAT IT CAN'T GET THROUGH!
TAKE THAT! AND THAT!
YOU'RE NO MATCH FOR THE POWER OF GRAVITY!
SQUELCH
SQUELCH
SQUELCH
COME ON, COME ON! WHY ISN'T THIS WORKING?
SQUELCH

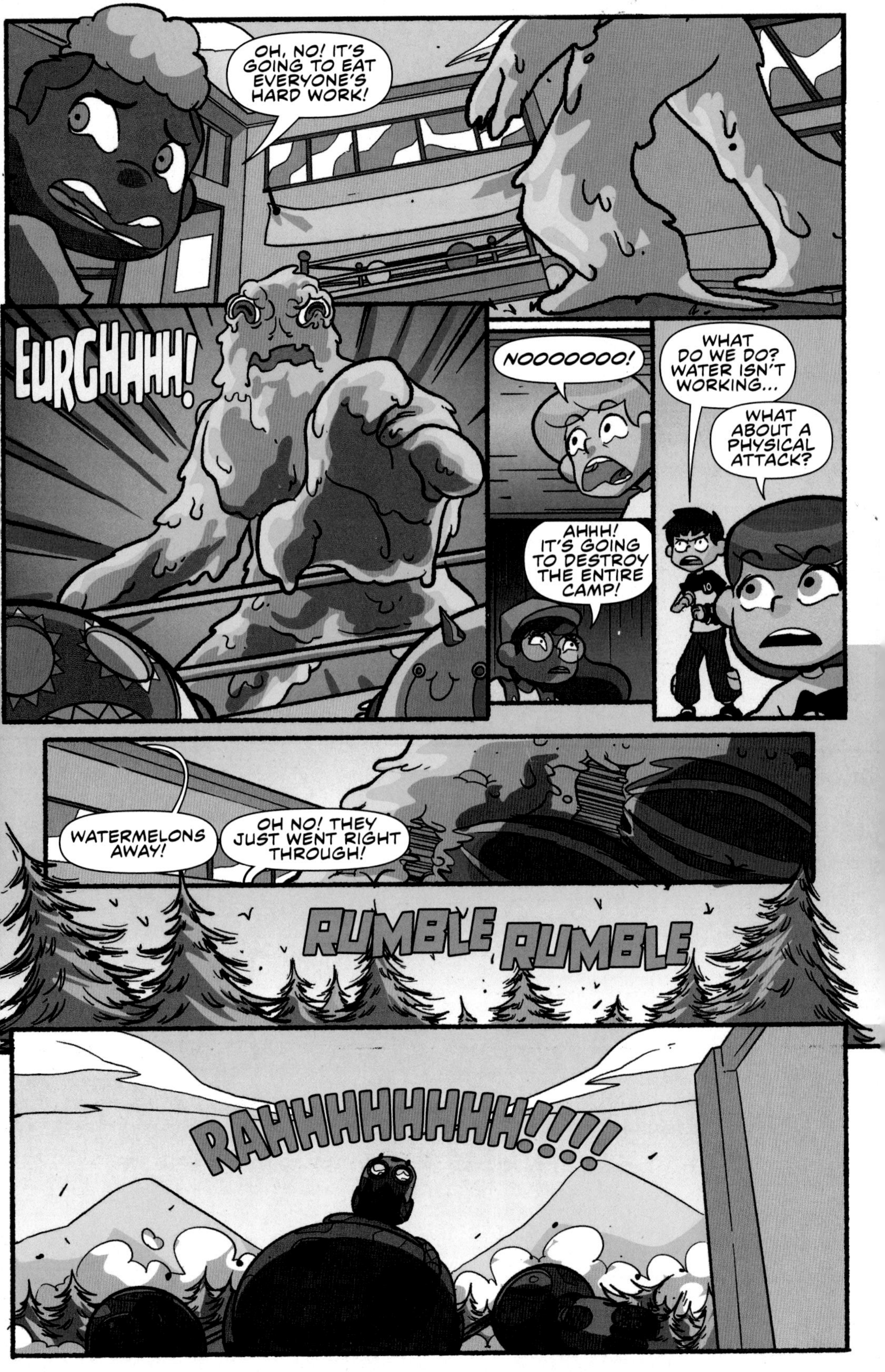
OH, NO! IT'S GOING TO EAT EVERYONE'S HARD WORK!
EURGHHHH!
NOOOOOOO!
AHHH! IT'S GOING TO DESTROY THE ENTIRE CAMP!
WHAT DO WE DO? WATER ISN'T WORKING...
WHAT ABOUT A PHYSICAL ATTACK?
WATERMELONS AWAY!
OH NO! THEY JUST WENT RIGHT THROUGH!
RUMBLE RUMBLE
RAHHHHHHHHH!!!!

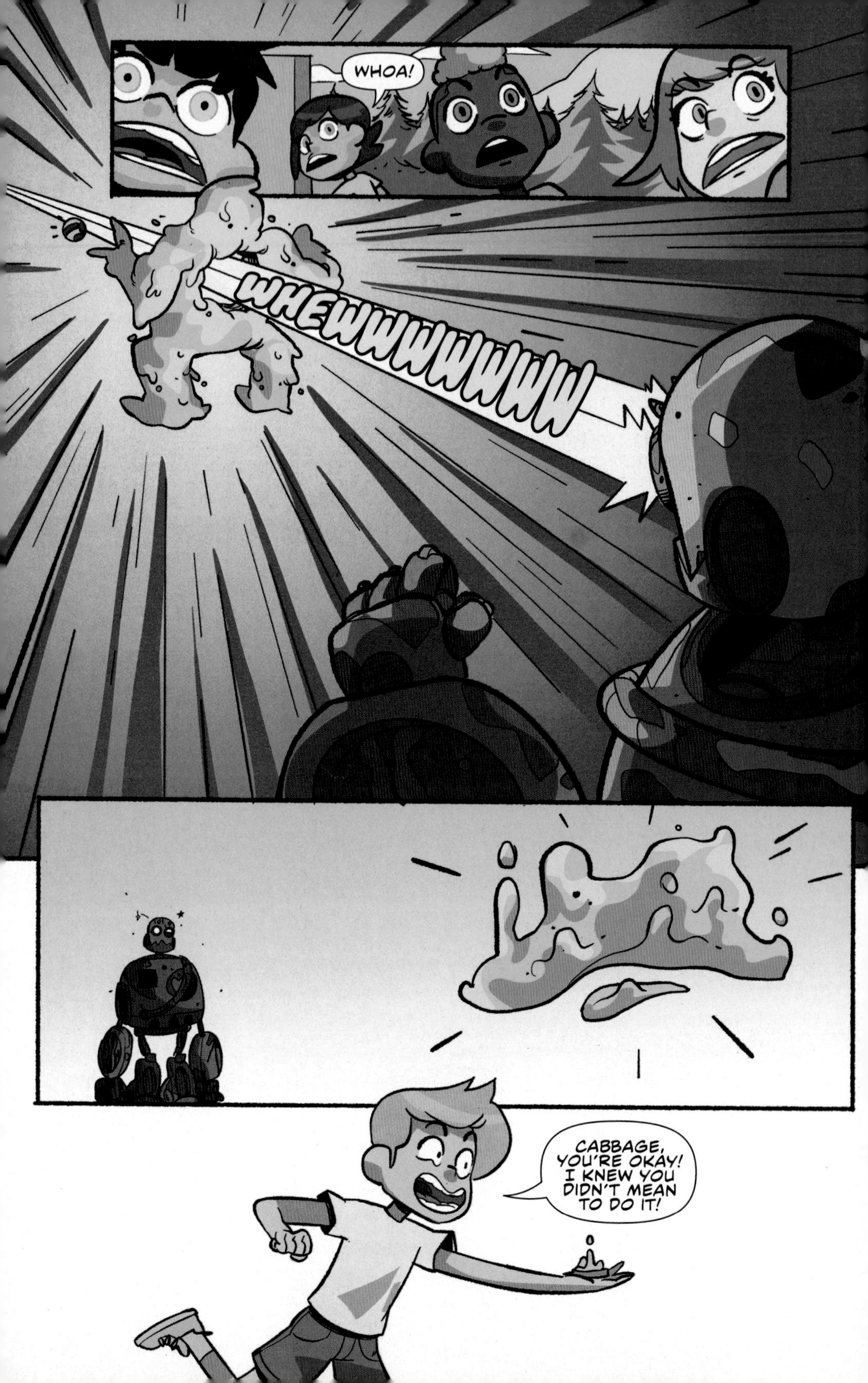
WHOA!
WHEWWWWWWWWW
CABBAGE, YOU'RE OKAY! I KNEW YOU DIDN'T MEAN TO DO IT!

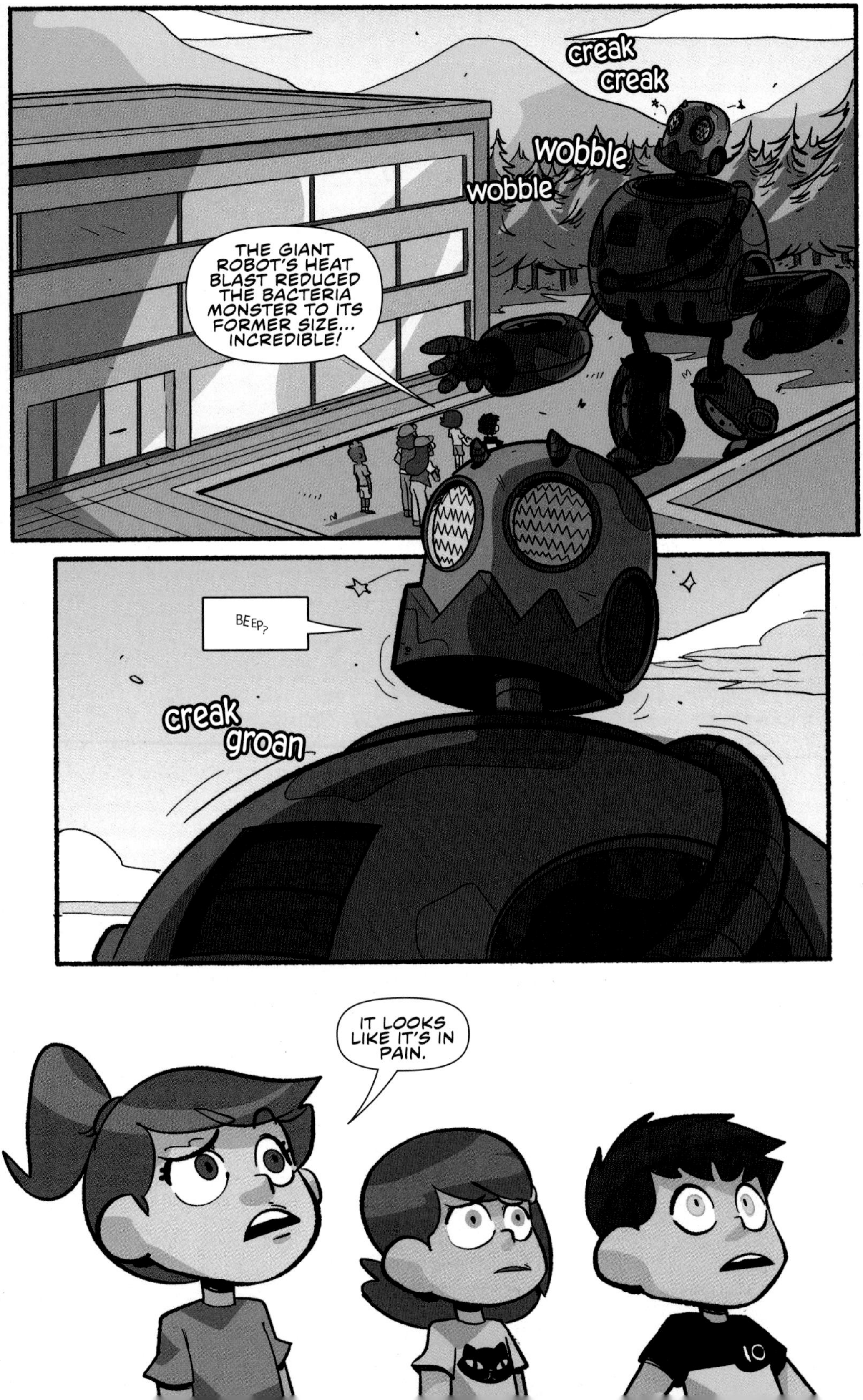
creak
creak
wobble
wobble
THE GIANT ROBOT'S HEAT BLAST REDUCED THE BACTERIA MONSTER TO ITS FORMER SIZE... INCREDIBLE!
BEEP?
creak
groan
IT LOOKS LIKE IT'S IN PAIN.

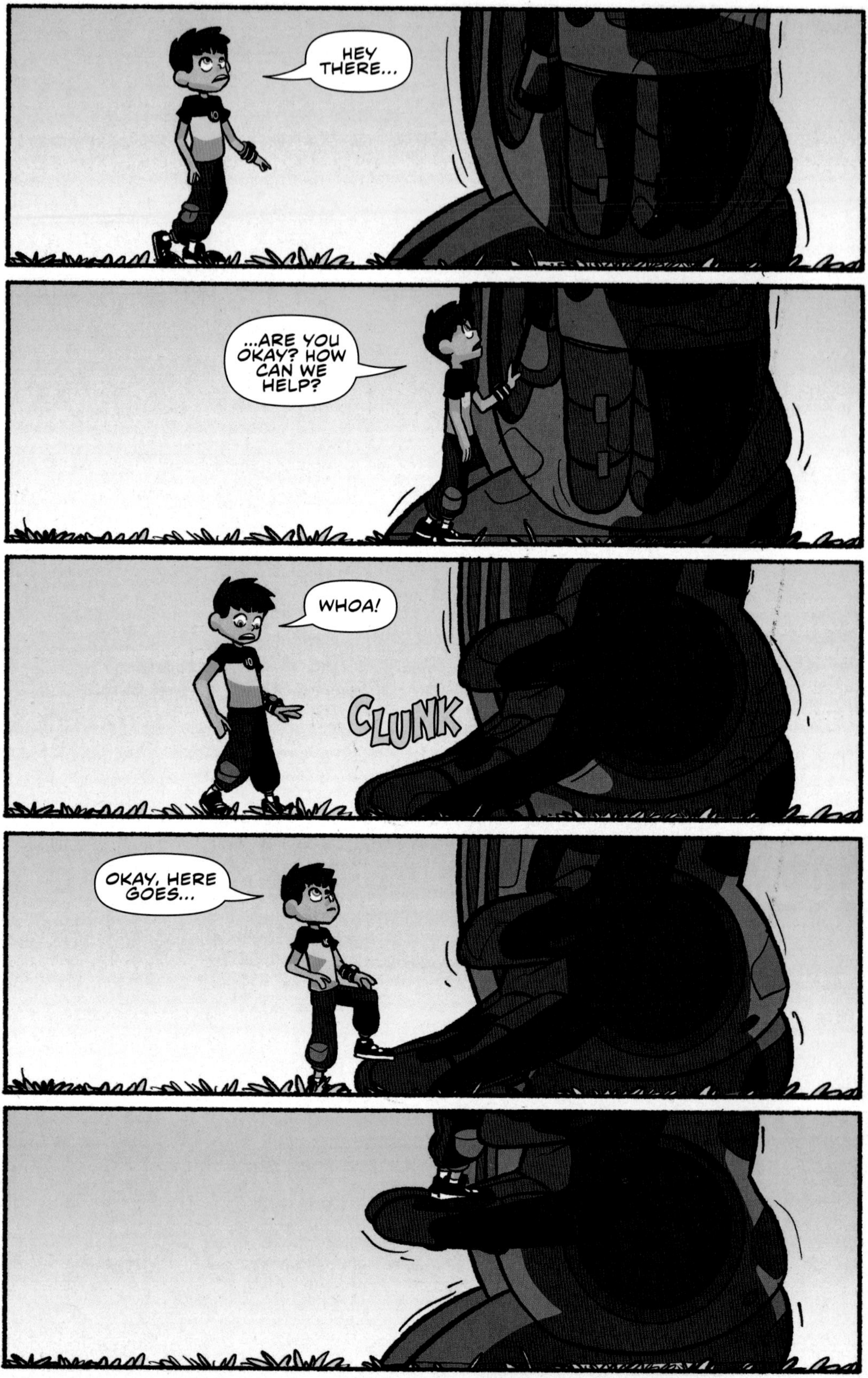
HEY THERE...
...ARE YOU OKAY? HOW CAN WE HELP?
WHOA!
CLUNK
OKAY, HERE GOES...

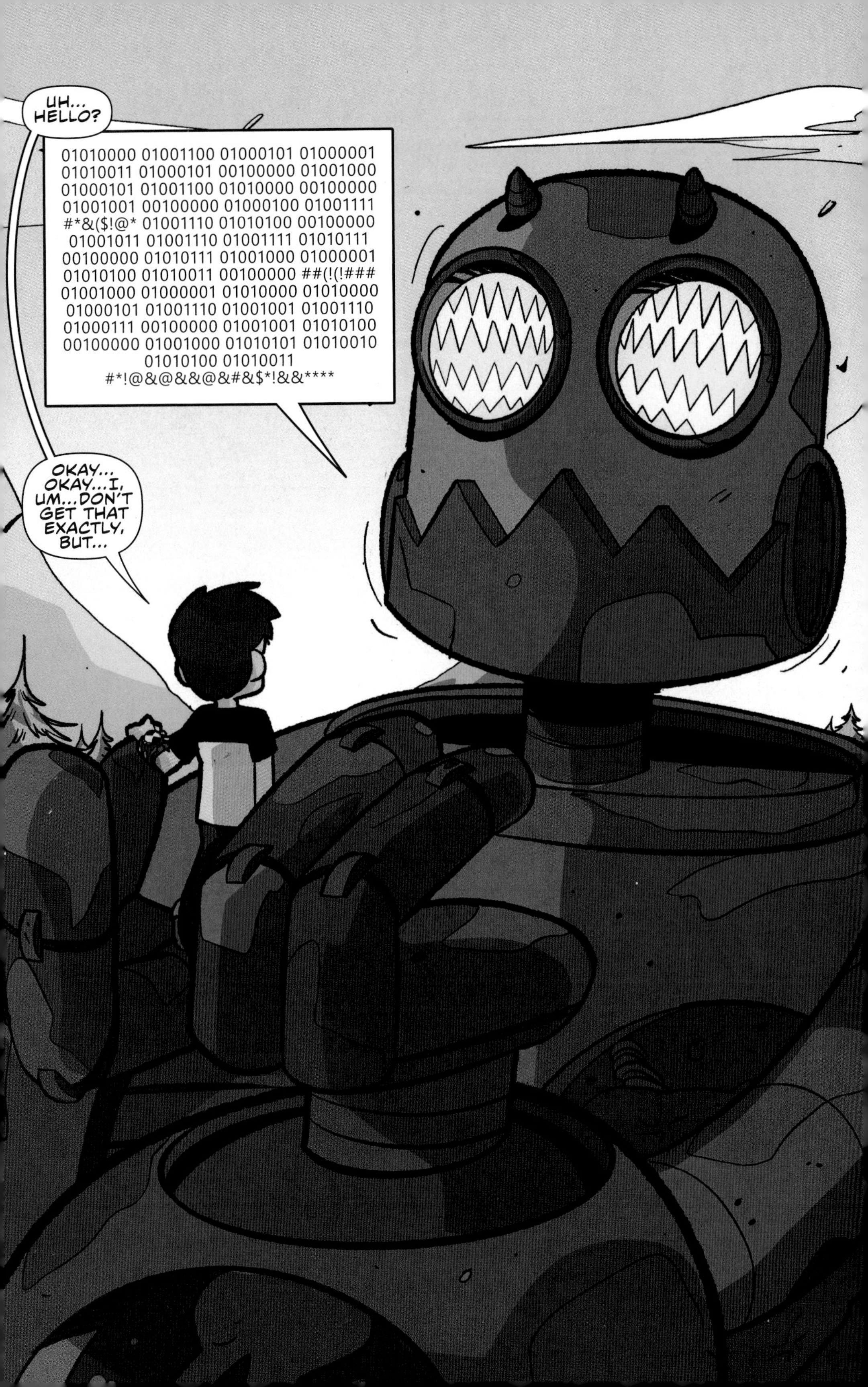
UH... HELLO?
01010000 01001100 01000101 01000001 01010011 01000101 00100000 01001000 01000101 01001100 01010000 00100000 01001001 00100000 01000100 01001111 #*&($!@* 01001110 01010100 00100000 01001011 01001110 01001111 01010111 00100000 01010111 01001000 01000001 01010100 01010011 00100000 ##(!(!### 01001000 01000001 01010000 01010000 01000101 01001110 01001001 01001110 01000111 00100000 01001001 01010100 00100000 01001000 01010101 01010010 01010100 01010011 #*!@&@&&@&#&$*!&&****
OKAY... OKAY...I, UM...DON'T GET THAT EXACTLY, BUT...

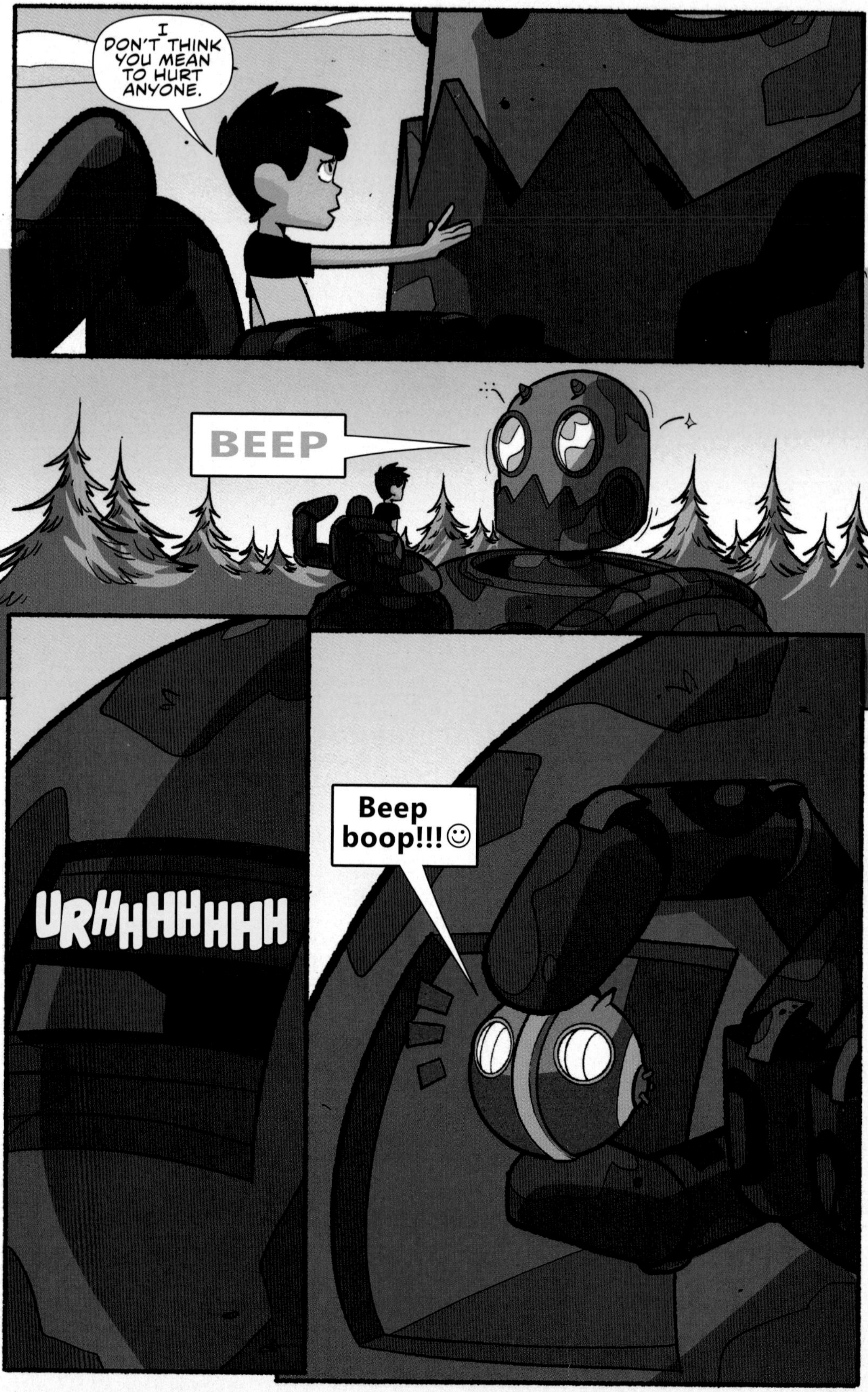
I DON'T THINK YOU MEAN TO HURT ANYONE.
BEEP
URHHHHHHH
Beep boop!!! ☺

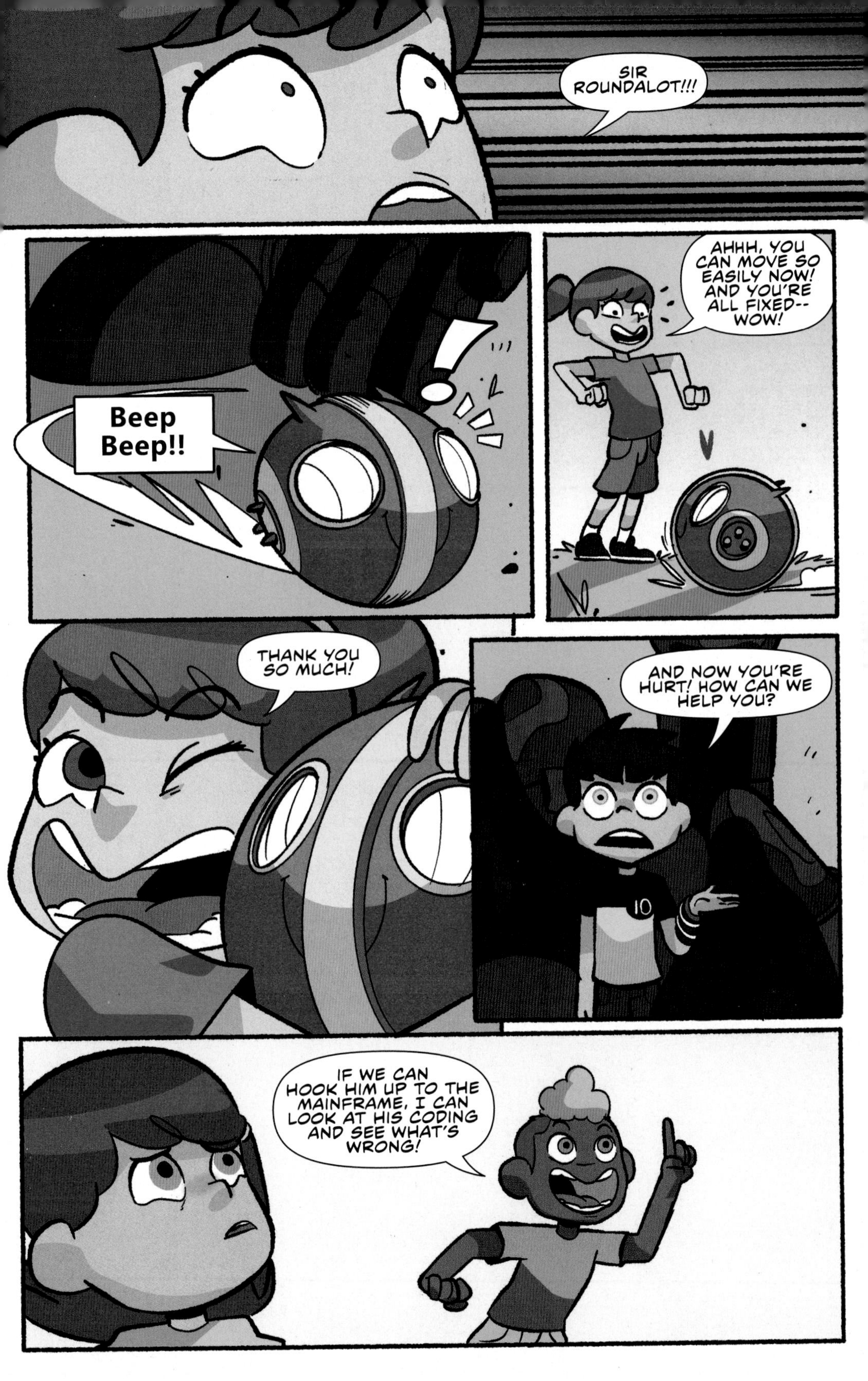
SIR ROUNDALOT!!!
Beep Beep!!
AHHH, YOU CAN MOVE SO EASILY NOW! AND YOU'RE ALL FIXED-- WOW!
THANK YOU SO MUCH!
AND NOW YOU'RE HURT! HOW CAN WE HELP YOU?
10
IF WE CAN HOOK HIM UP TO THE MAINFRAME, I CAN LOOK AT HIS CODING AND SEE WHAT'S WRONG!

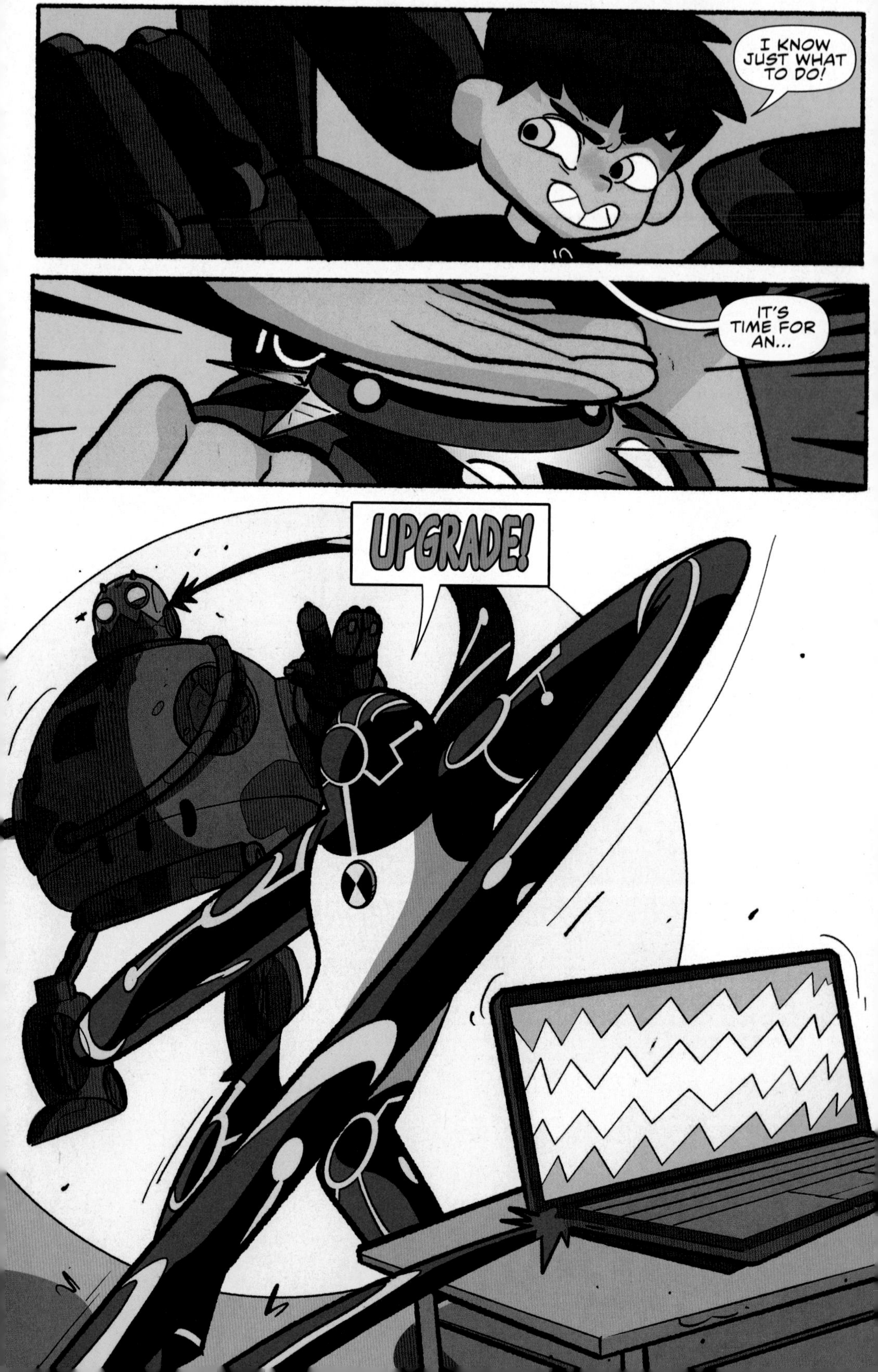
I KNOW JUST WHAT TO DO!
IT'S TIME FOR AN...
UPGRADE!

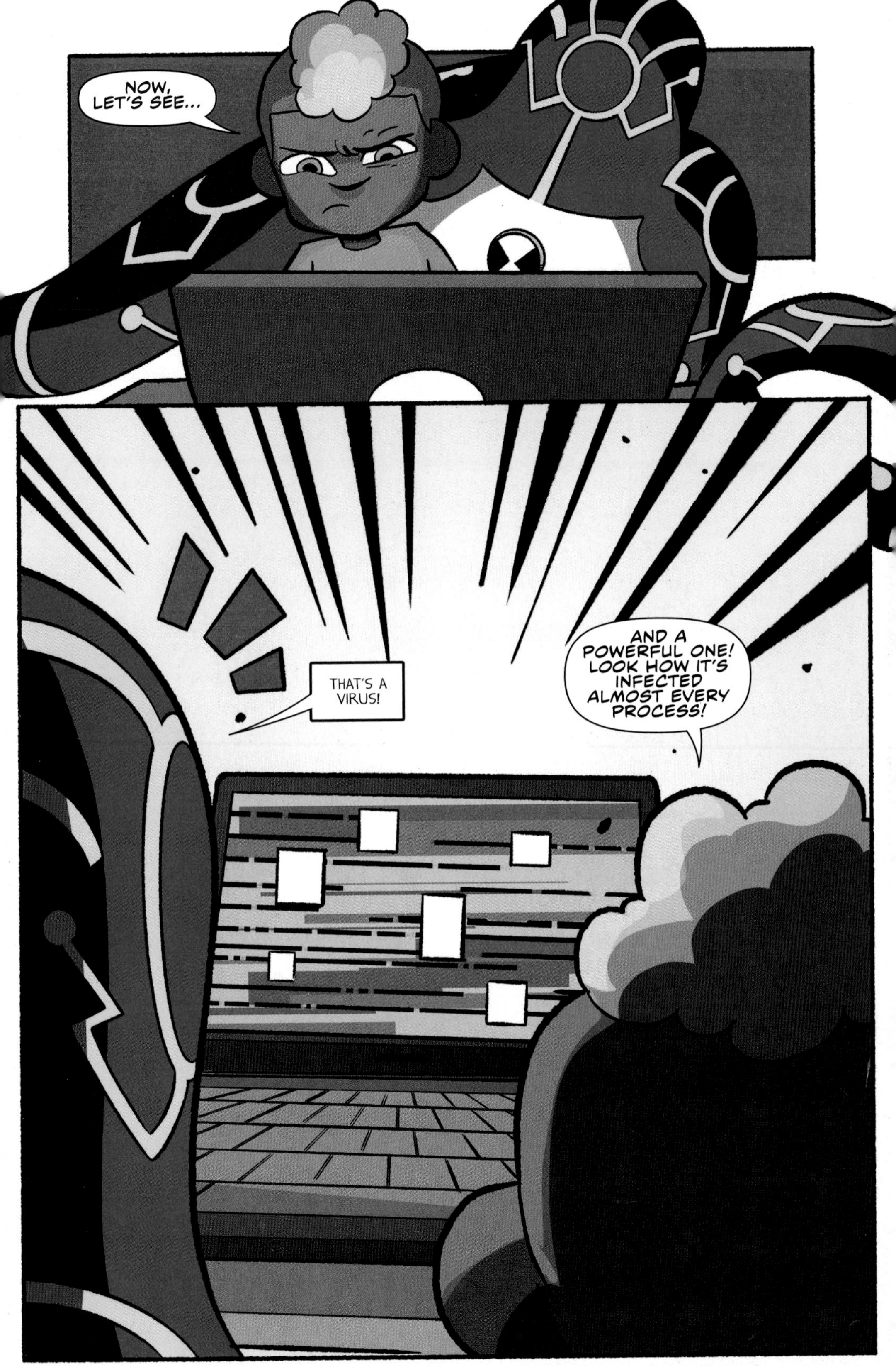
NOW, LET'S SEE...
THAT'S A VIRUS!
AND A POWERFUL ONE! LOOK HOW IT'S INFECTED ALMOST EVERY PROCESS!

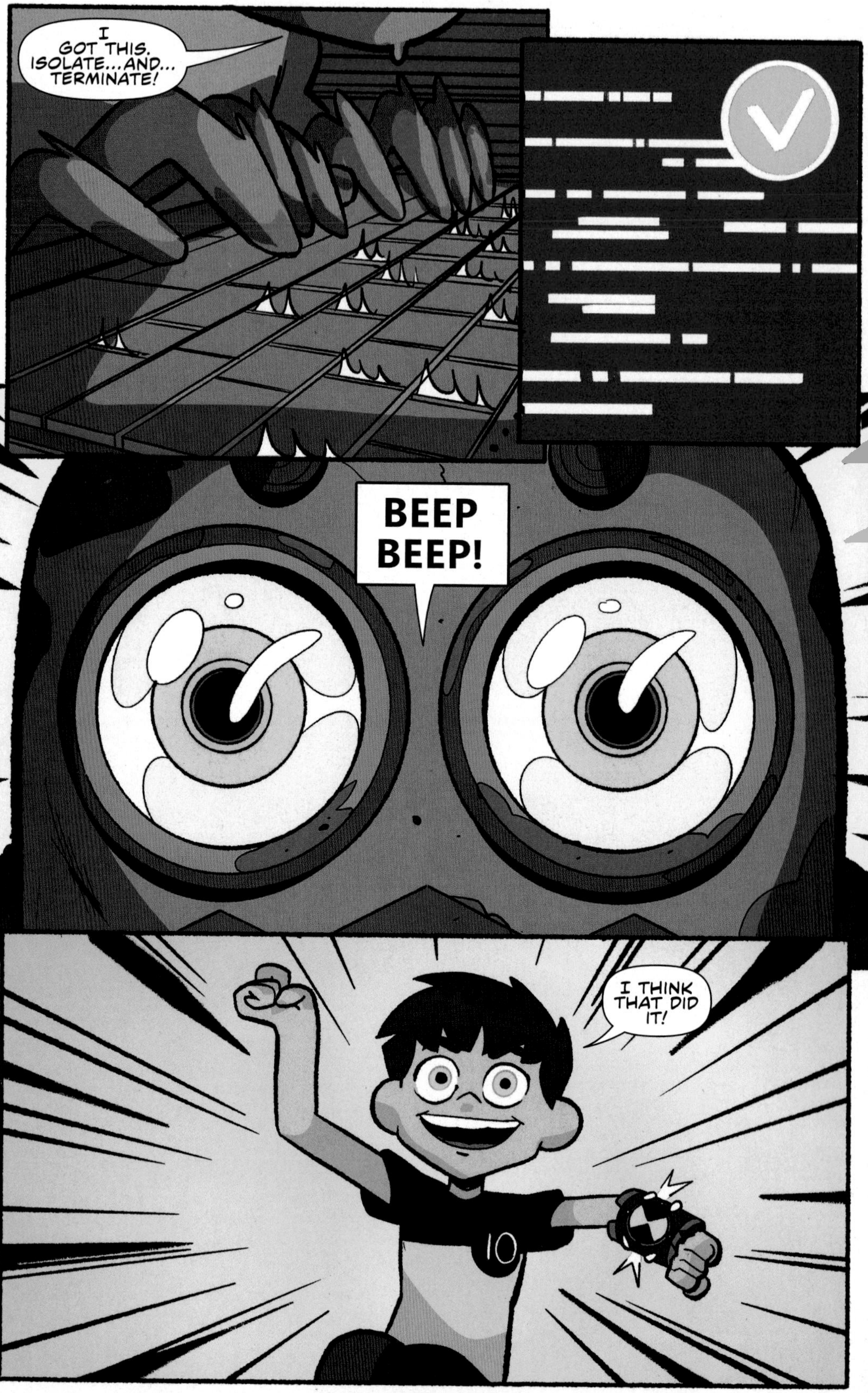
I GOT THIS. ISOLATE...AND... TERMINATE!
BEEP BEEP!
I THINK THAT DID IT!
10

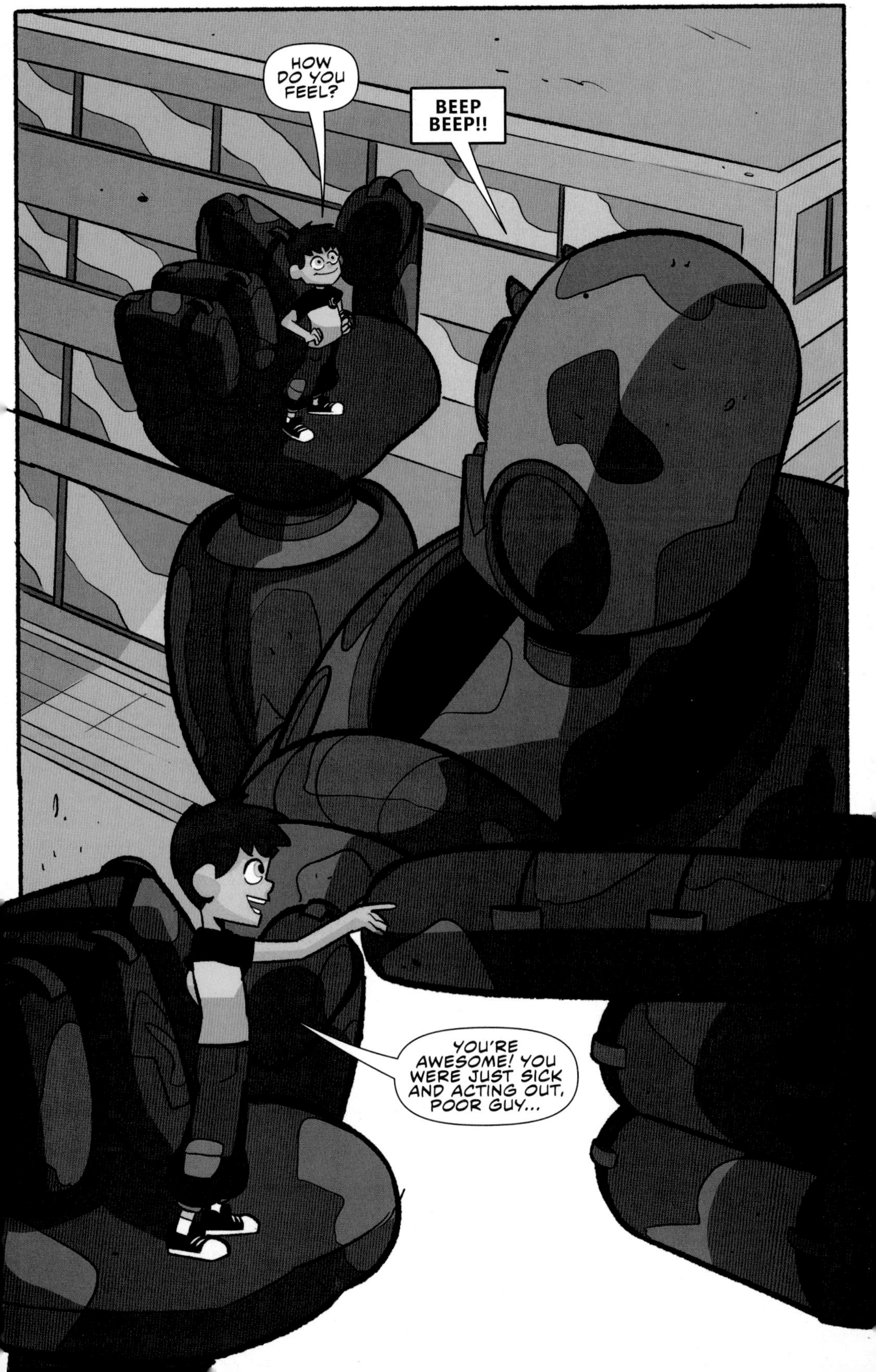
HOW DO YOU FEEL?
BEEP BEEP!!
YOU'RE AWESOME! YOU WERE JUST SICK AND ACTING OUT, POOR GUY...

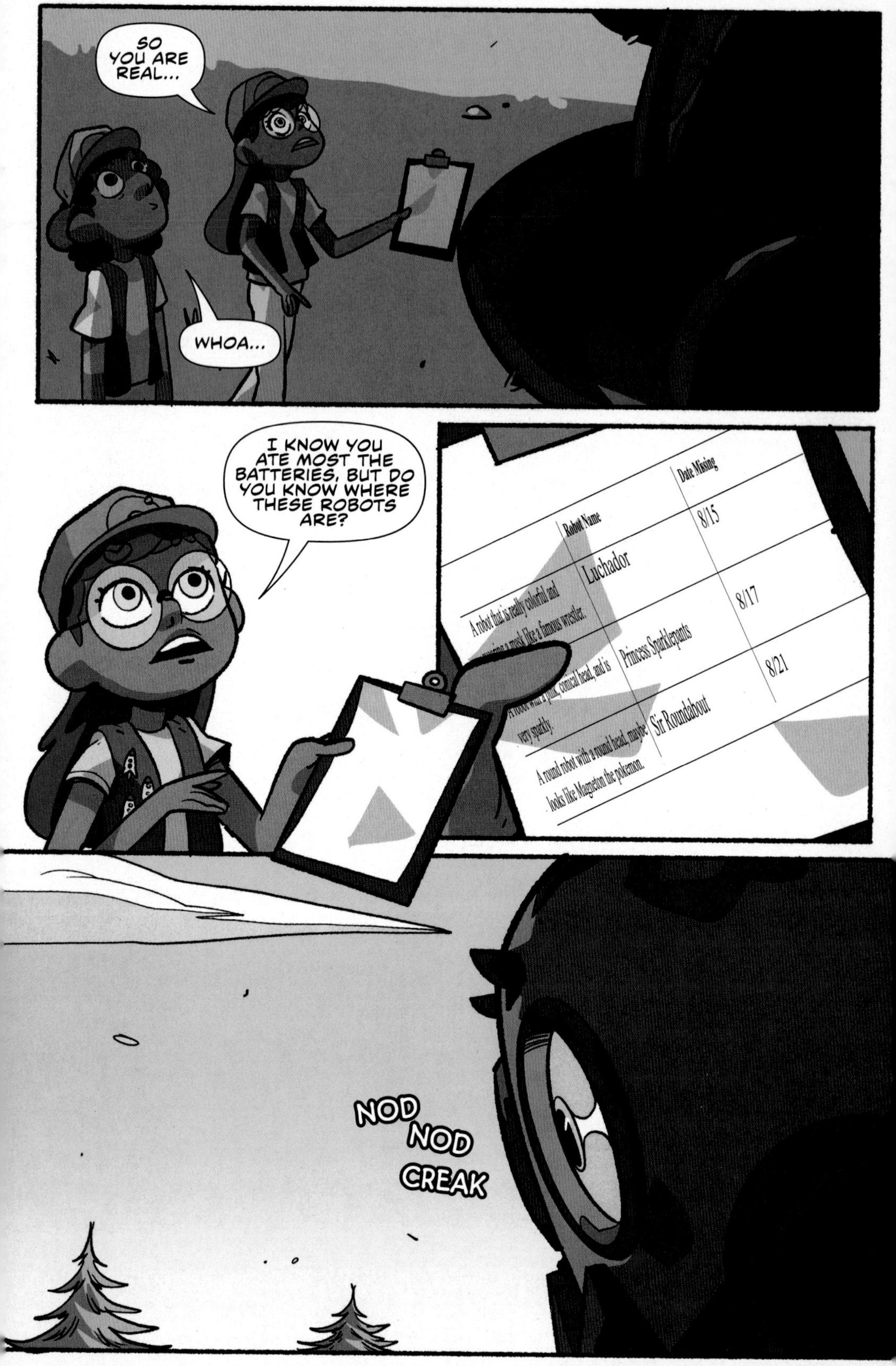
SO YOU ARE REAL...
WHOA...
I KNOW YOU ATE MOST THE BATTERIES, BUT DO YOU KNOW WHERE THESE ROBOTS ARE?
Robot Name
Date Missing
A robot that is really colorful and
a mask like a famous wrestler.
Luchador
8/15
conical head, and is
very sparkly.
Princess Sparklepants
8/17
A round robot with a round head, maybe looks like Magneton the pokemon.
Sir Roundabout
8/21
NOD
NOD
CREAK

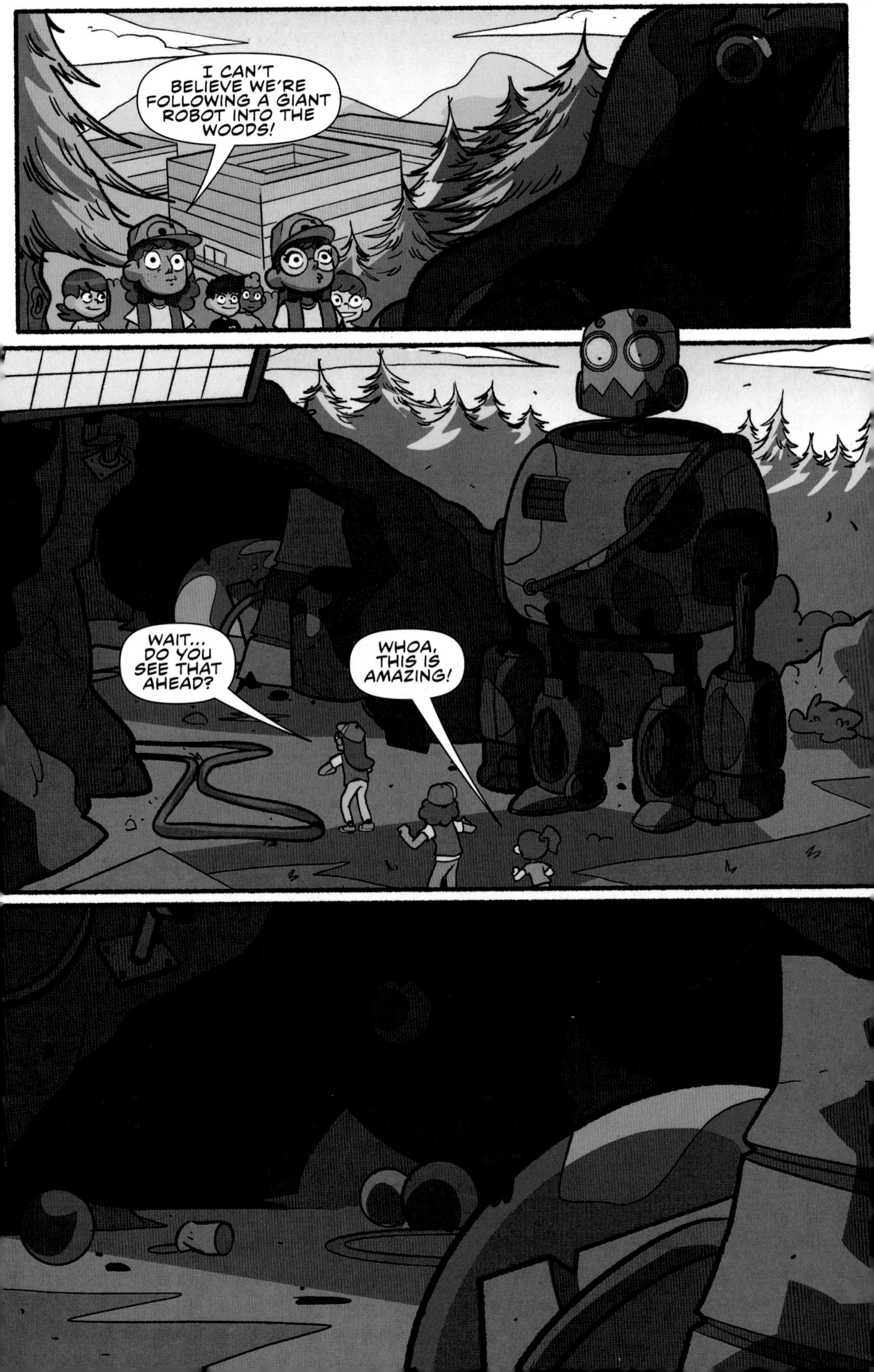
I CAN'T BELIEVE WE'RE FOLLOWING A GIANT ROBOT INTO THE WOODS!
WAIT... DO YOU SEE THAT AHEAD?
WHOA, THIS IS AMAZING!

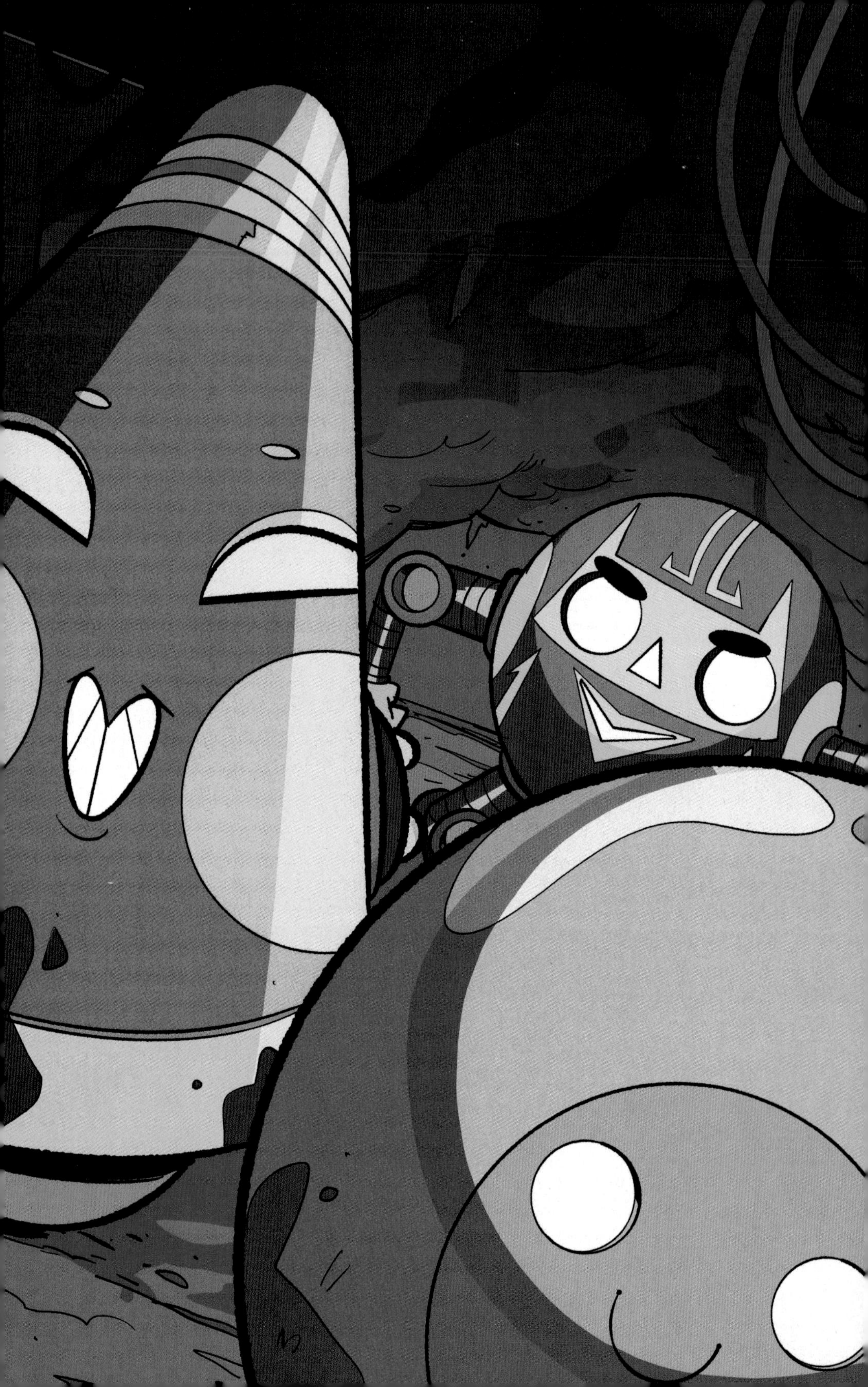

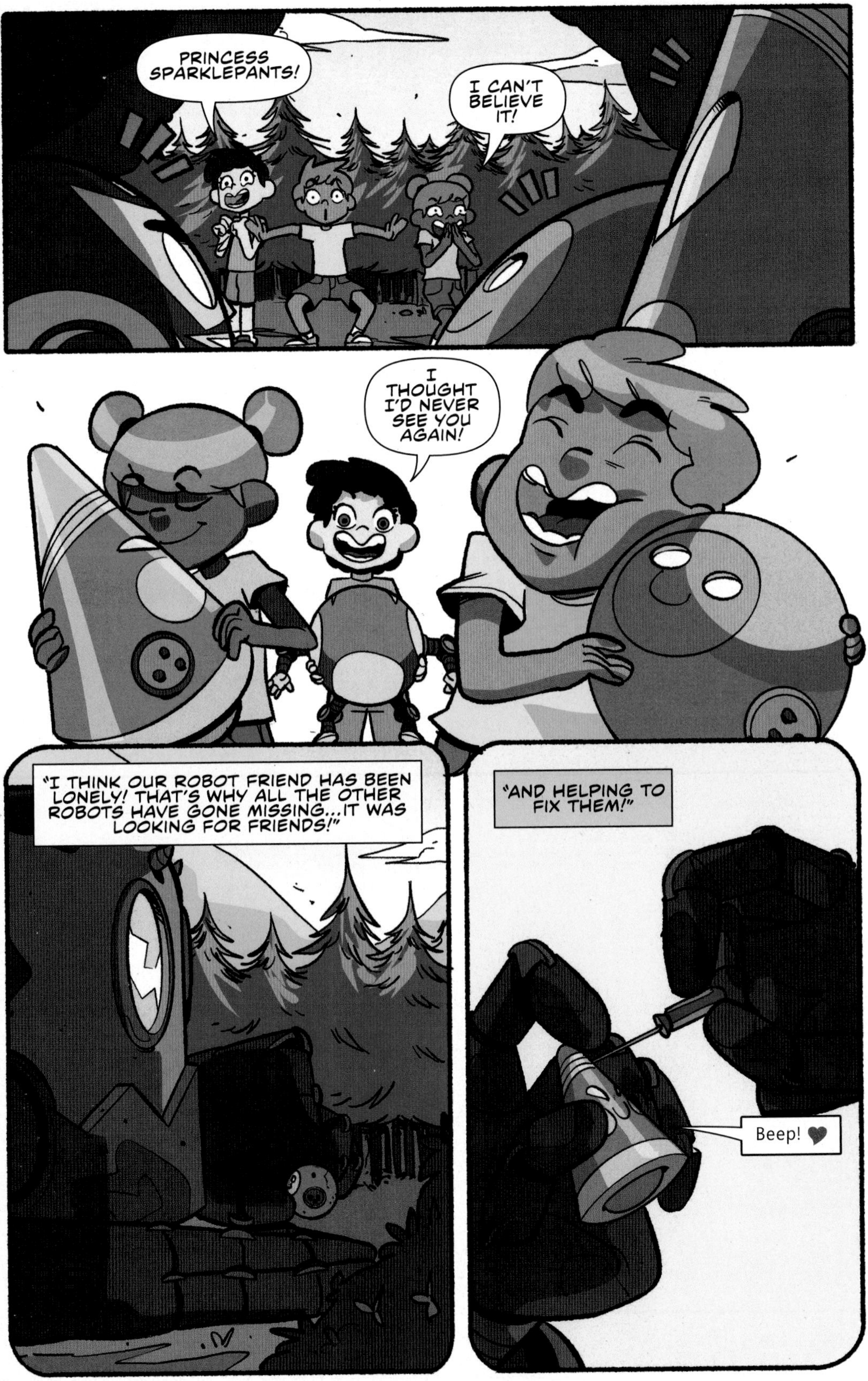
PRINCESS SPARKLEPANTS!
I CAN'T BELIEVE IT!
I THOUGHT I'D NEVER SEE YOU AGAIN!
"I THINK OUR ROBOT FRIEND HAS BEEN LONELY! THAT'S WHY ALL THE OTHER ROBOTS HAVE GONE MISSING...IT WAS LOOKING FOR FRIENDS!"
"AND HELPING TO FIX THEM!"
Beep! ♥

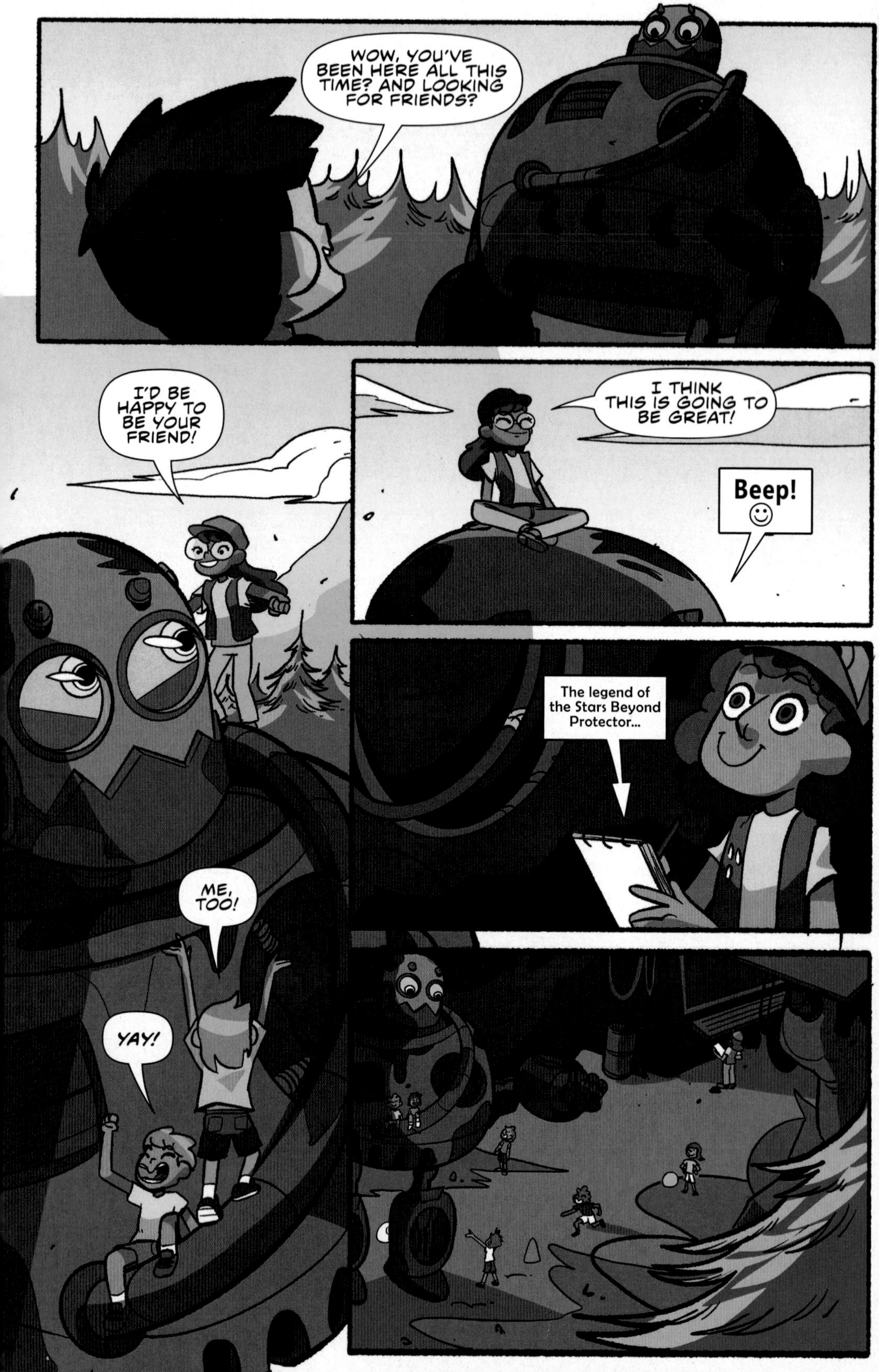
WOW, YOU'VE BEEN HERE ALL THIS TIME? AND LOOKING FOR FRIENDS?
I'D BE HAPPY TO BE YOUR FRIEND!
I THINK THIS IS GOING TO BE GREAT!
Beep! ☺
ME, TOO!
YAY!
The legend of the Stars Beyond Protector...

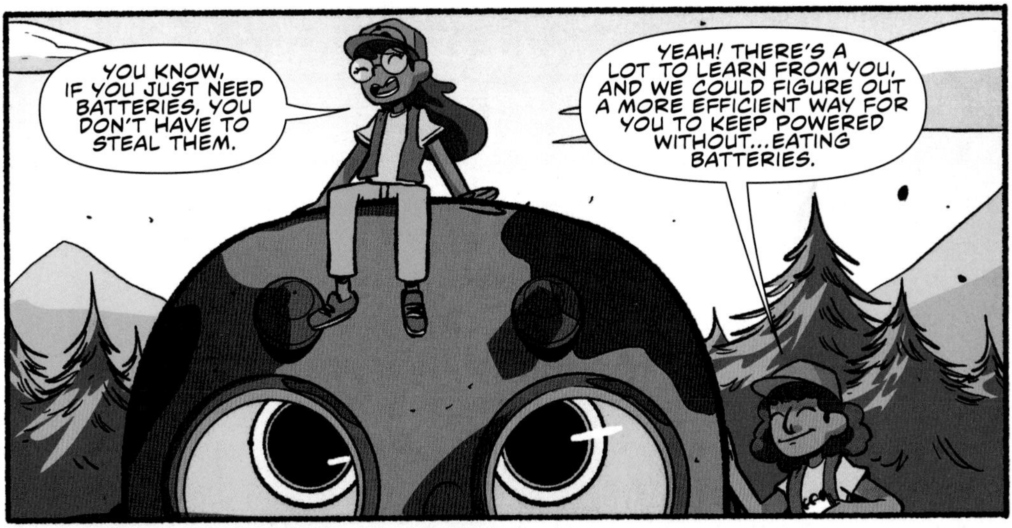
YOU KNOW, IF YOU JUST NEED BATTERIES, YOU DON'T HAVE TO STEAL THEM.
YEAH! THERE'S A LOT TO LEARN FROM YOU, AND WE COULD FIGURE OUT A MORE EFFICIENT WAY FOR YOU TO KEEP POWERED WITHOUT...EATING BATTERIES.

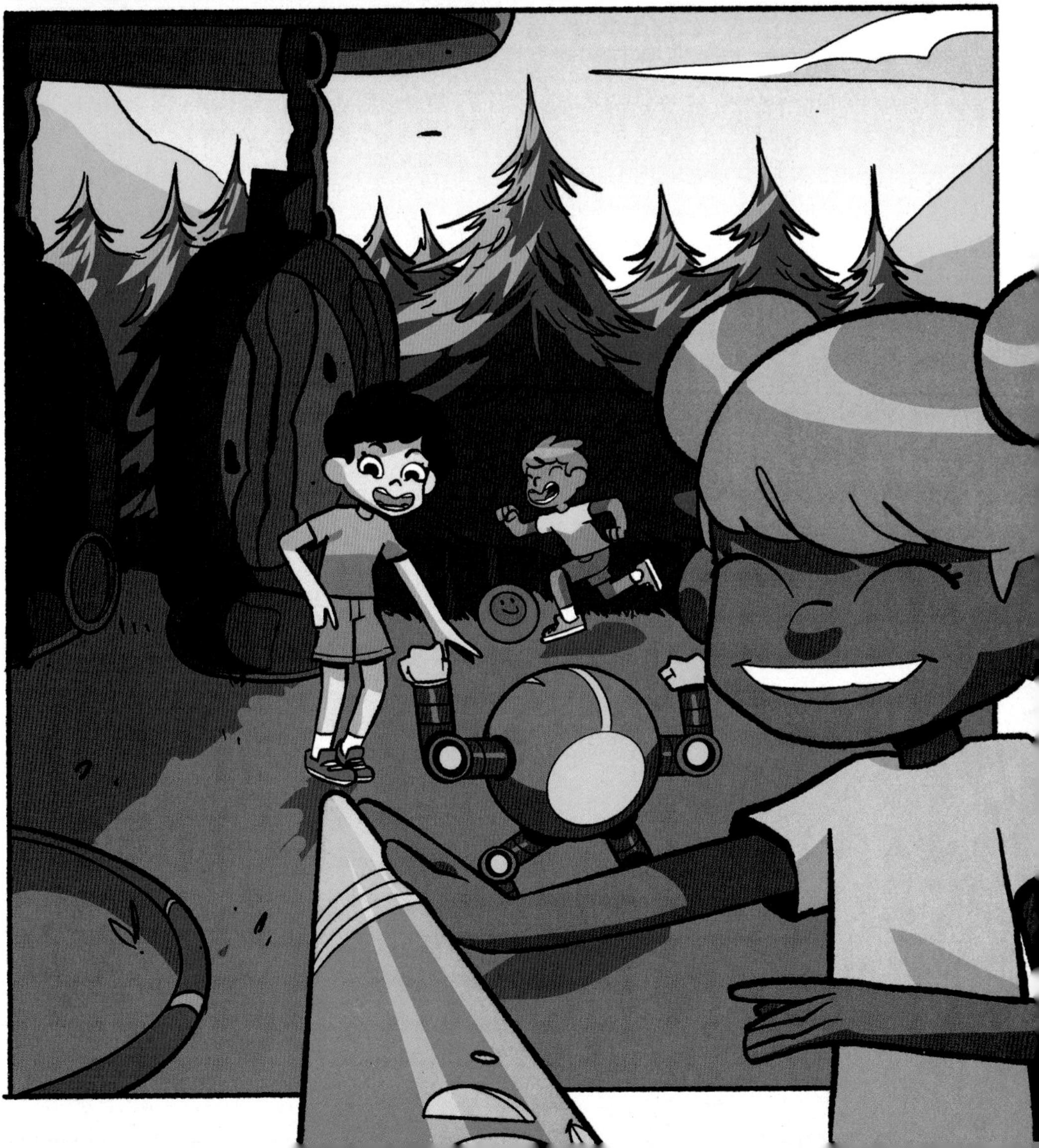

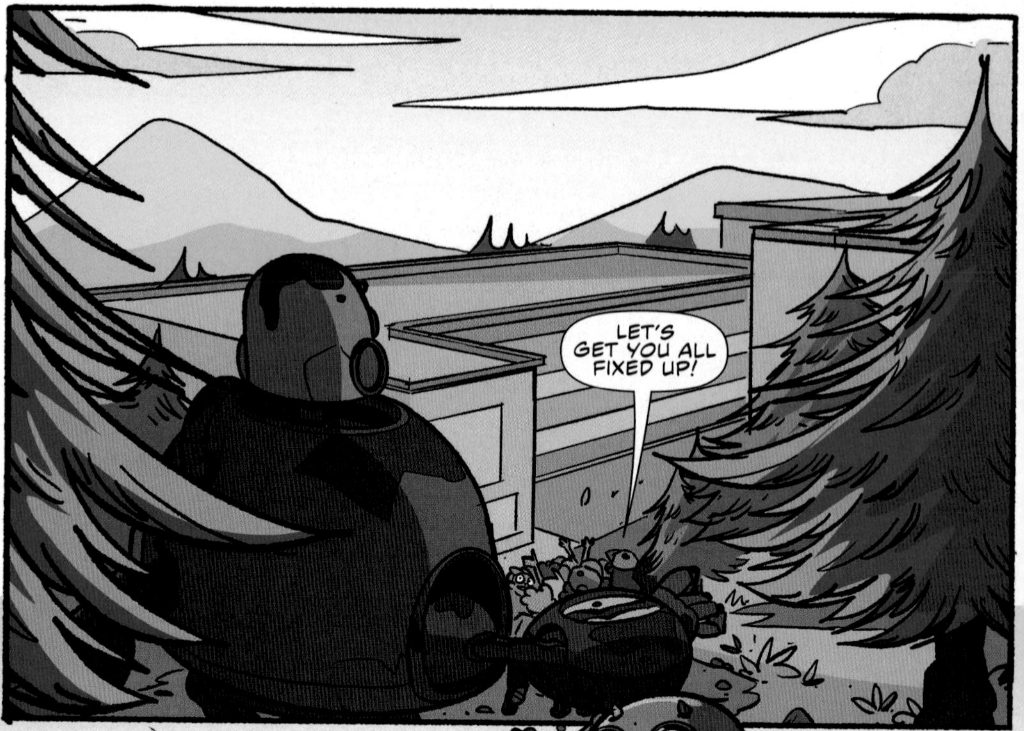
LET'S GET YOU ALL FIXED UP!

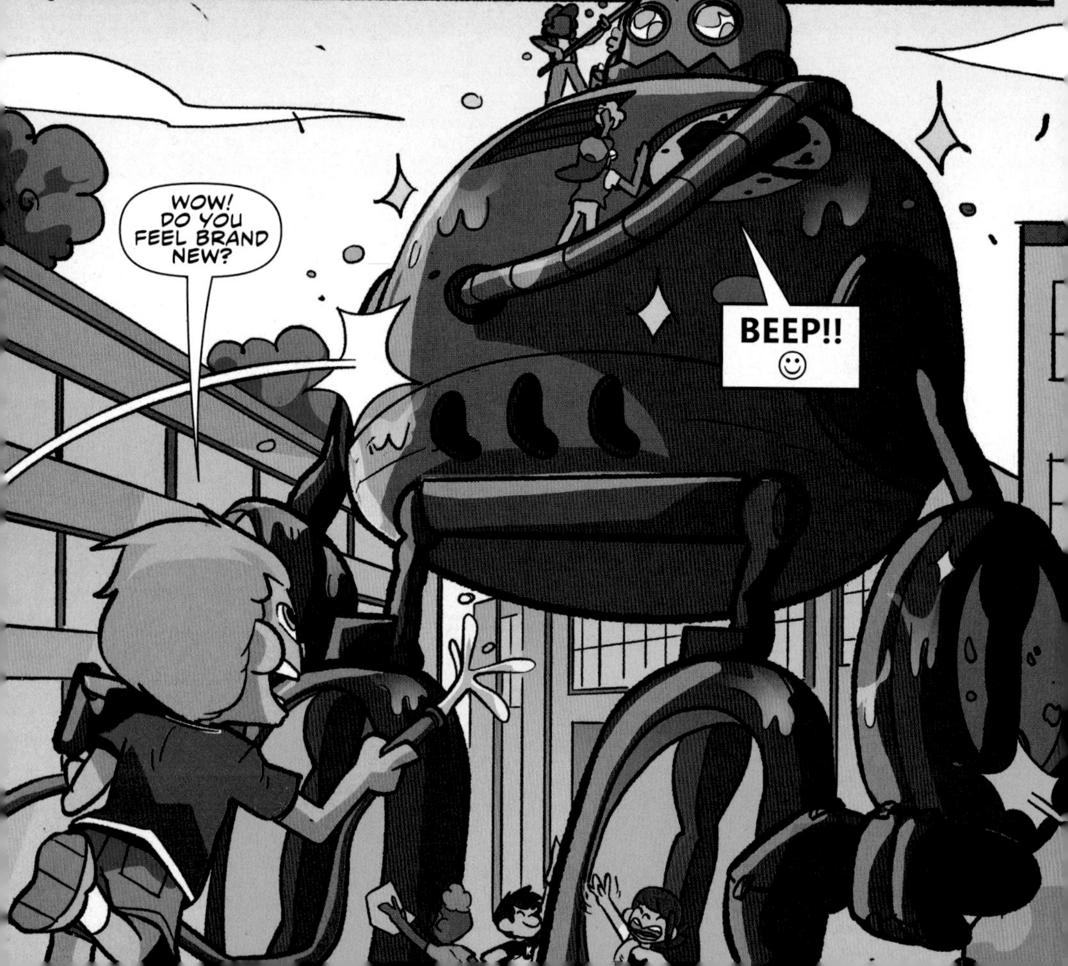
WOW! DO YOU FEEL BRAND NEW?
BEEP!! ☺

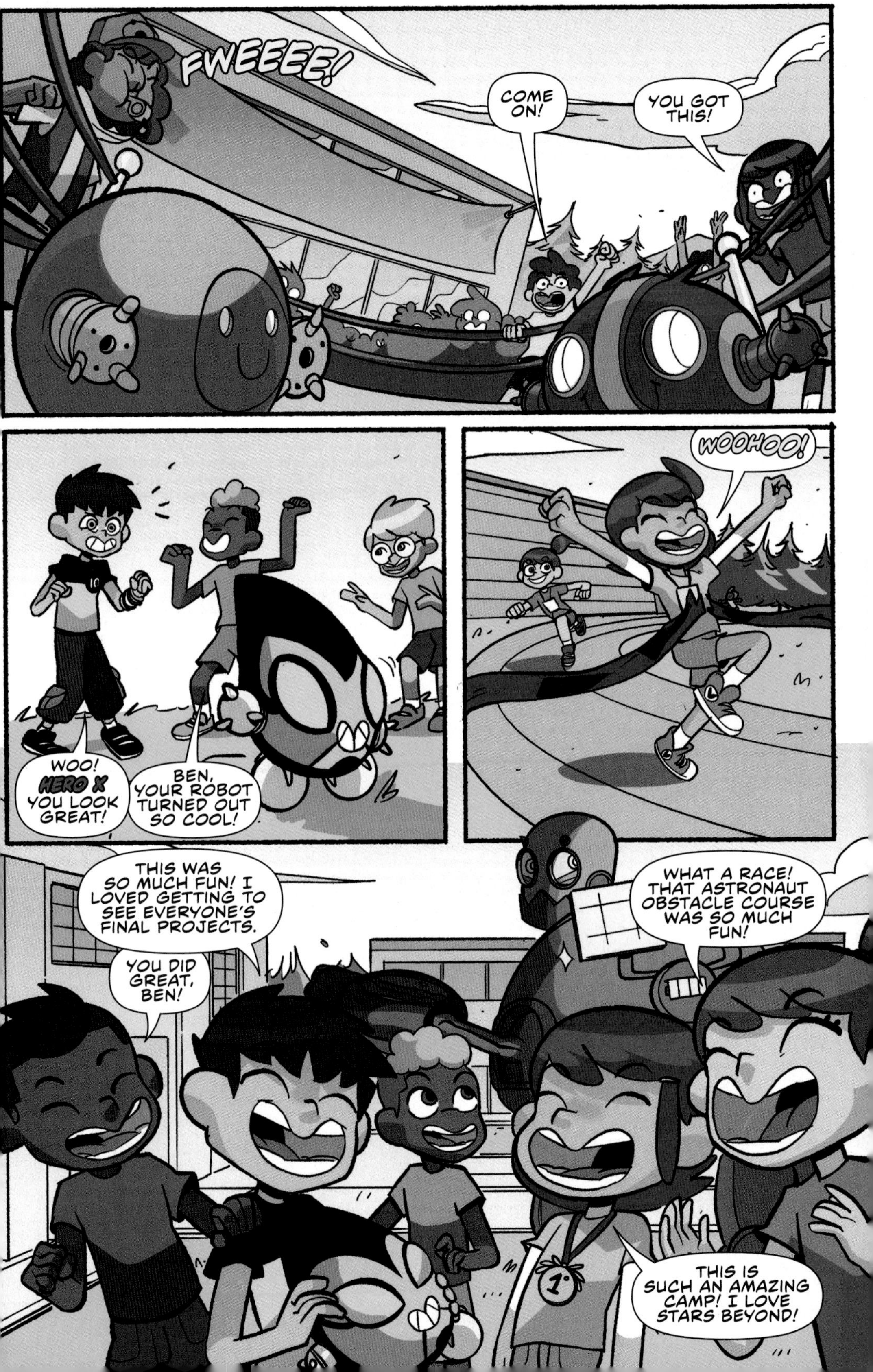
FWEEEEE!
COME ON!
YOU GOT THIS!
WOO! HERO X YOU LOOK GREAT!
BEN, YOUR ROBOT TURNED OUT SO COOL!
WOOHOO!
THIS WAS SO MUCH FUN! I LOVED GETTING TO SEE EVERYONE'S FINAL PROJECTS.
YOU DID GREAT, BEN!
WHAT A RACE! THAT ASTRONAUT OBSTACLE COURSE WAS SO MUCH FUN!
THIS IS SUCH AN AMAZING CAMP! I LOVE STARS BEYOND!

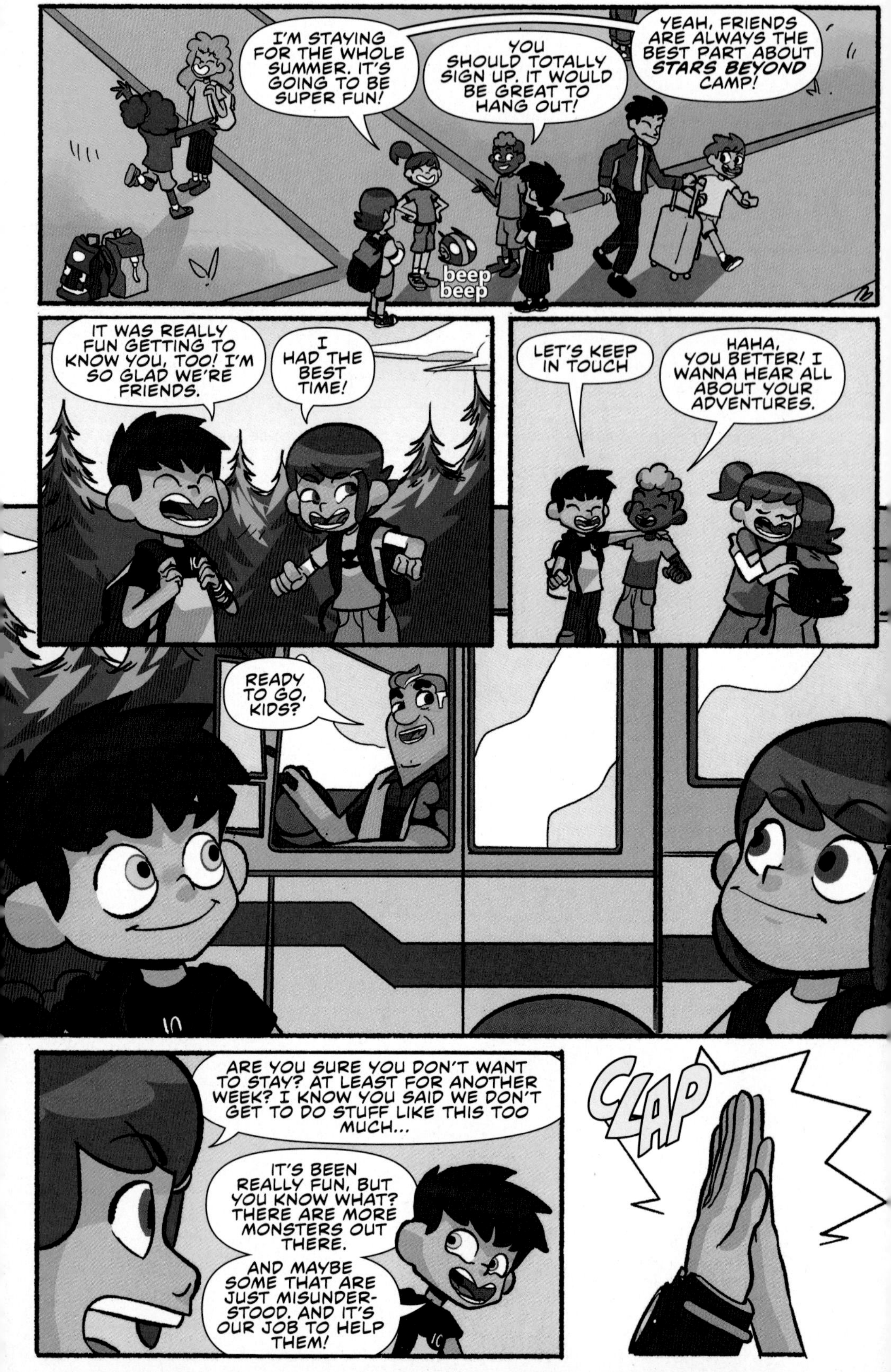
I'M STAYING FOR THE WHOLE SUMMER. IT'S GOING TO BE SUPER FUN!
YOU SHOULD TOTALLY SIGN UP. IT WOULD BE GREAT TO HANG OUT!
YEAH, FRIENDS ARE ALWAYS THE BEST PART ABOUT **STARS BEYOND** CAMP!
beep beep
IT WAS REALLY FUN GETTING TO KNOW YOU, TOO! I'M SO GLAD WE'RE FRIENDS.
I HAD THE BEST TIME!
LET'S KEEP IN TOUCH
HAHA, YOU BETTER! I WANNA HEAR ALL ABOUT YOUR ADVENTURES.
READY TO GO, KIDS?
ARE YOU SURE YOU DON'T WANT TO STAY? AT LEAST FOR ANOTHER WEEK? I KNOW YOU SAID WE DON'T GET TO DO STUFF LIKE THIS TOO MUCH...
IT'S BEEN REALLY FUN, BUT YOU KNOW WHAT? THERE ARE MORE MONSTERS OUT THERE.
AND MAYBE SOME THAT ARE JUST MISUNDER-STOOD. AND IT'S OUR JOB TO HELP THEM!
CLAP

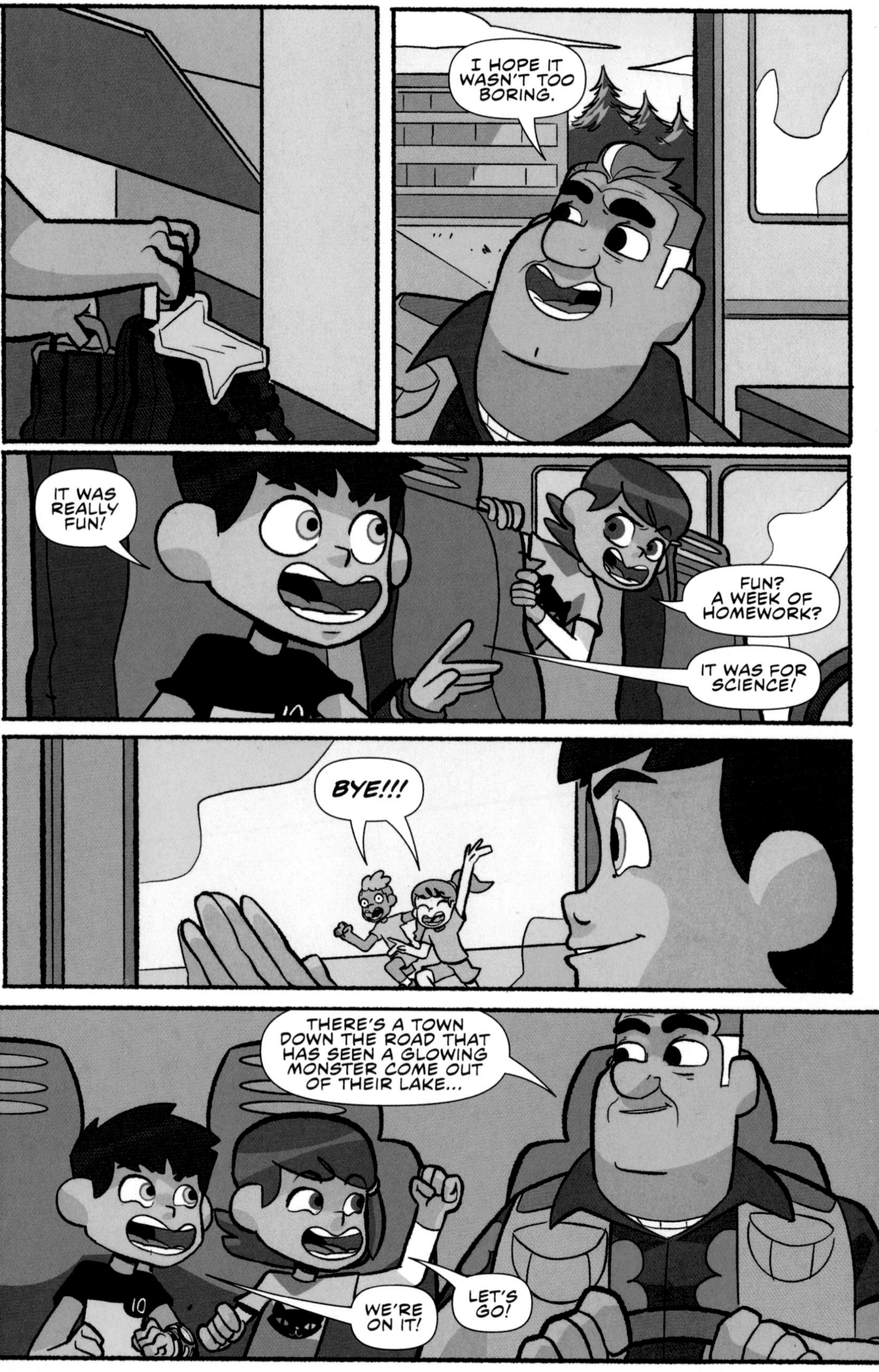
I HOPE IT WASN'T TOO BORING.
IT WAS REALLY FUN!
FUN? A WEEK OF HOMEWORK?
IT WAS FOR SCIENCE!
BYE!!!
THERE'S A TOWN DOWN THE ROAD THAT HAS SEEN A GLOWING MONSTER COME OUT OF THEIR LAKE...
WE'RE ON IT!
LET'S GO!
10

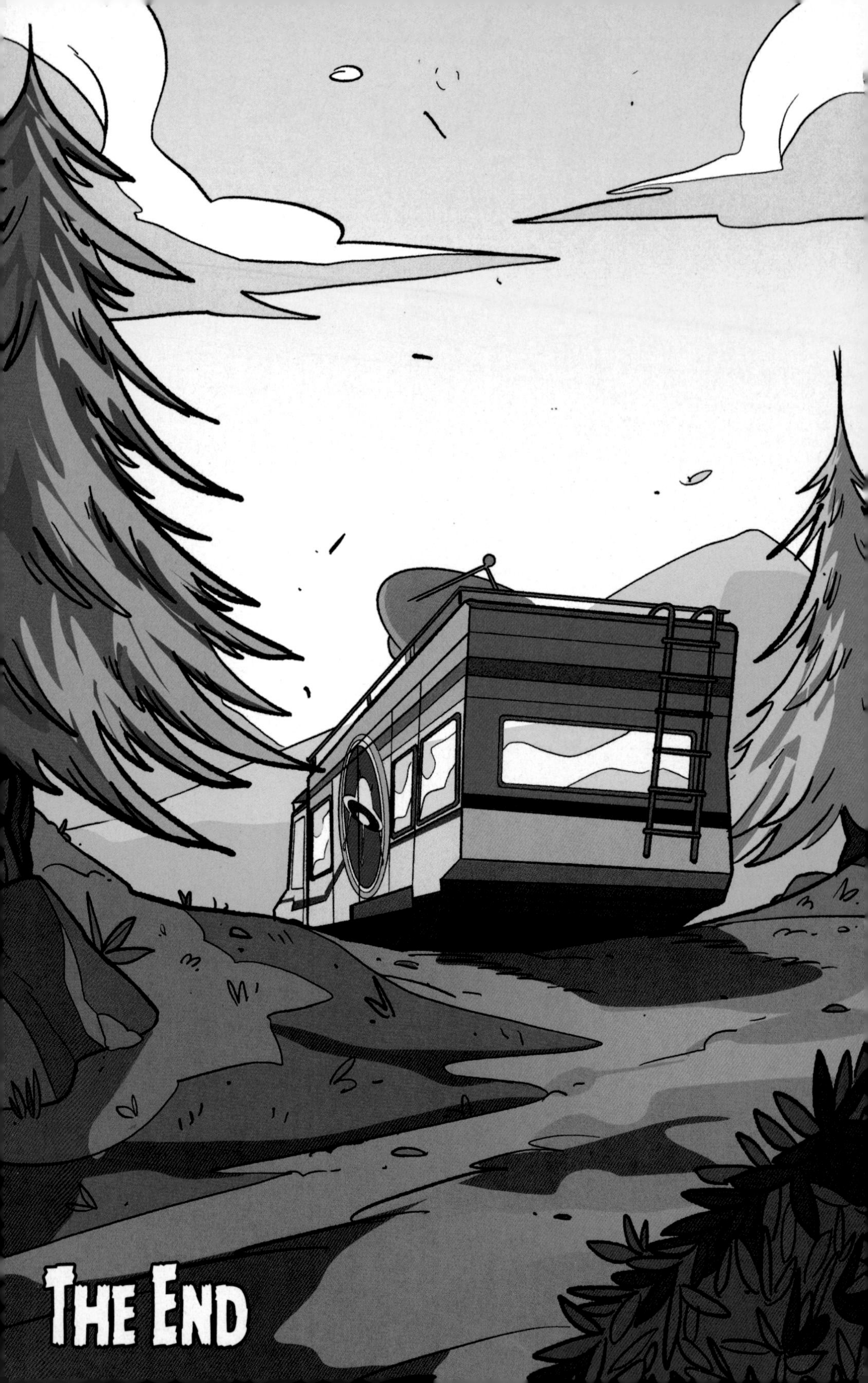
THE END

BEN'S ADVENTURES IN THE RUSTBUCKET CONTINUE IN...

"MECHA MADNESS"

AVAILABLE FALL 2019

CN
BEN 10
MECHA MADNESS
BONUS STICKERS INSIDE
BEN 10™
MECHA MADNESS
C.B. LEE
LIDAN CHEN
kaboom!

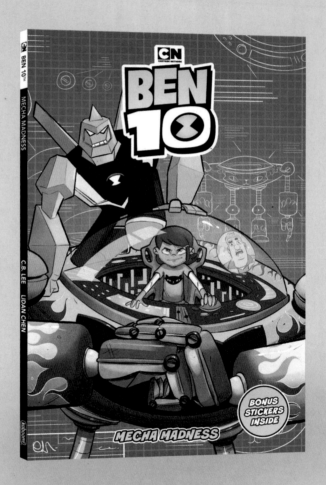

WRITTEN BY

C.B. LEE

ILLUSTRATED BY

LIDAN CHEN

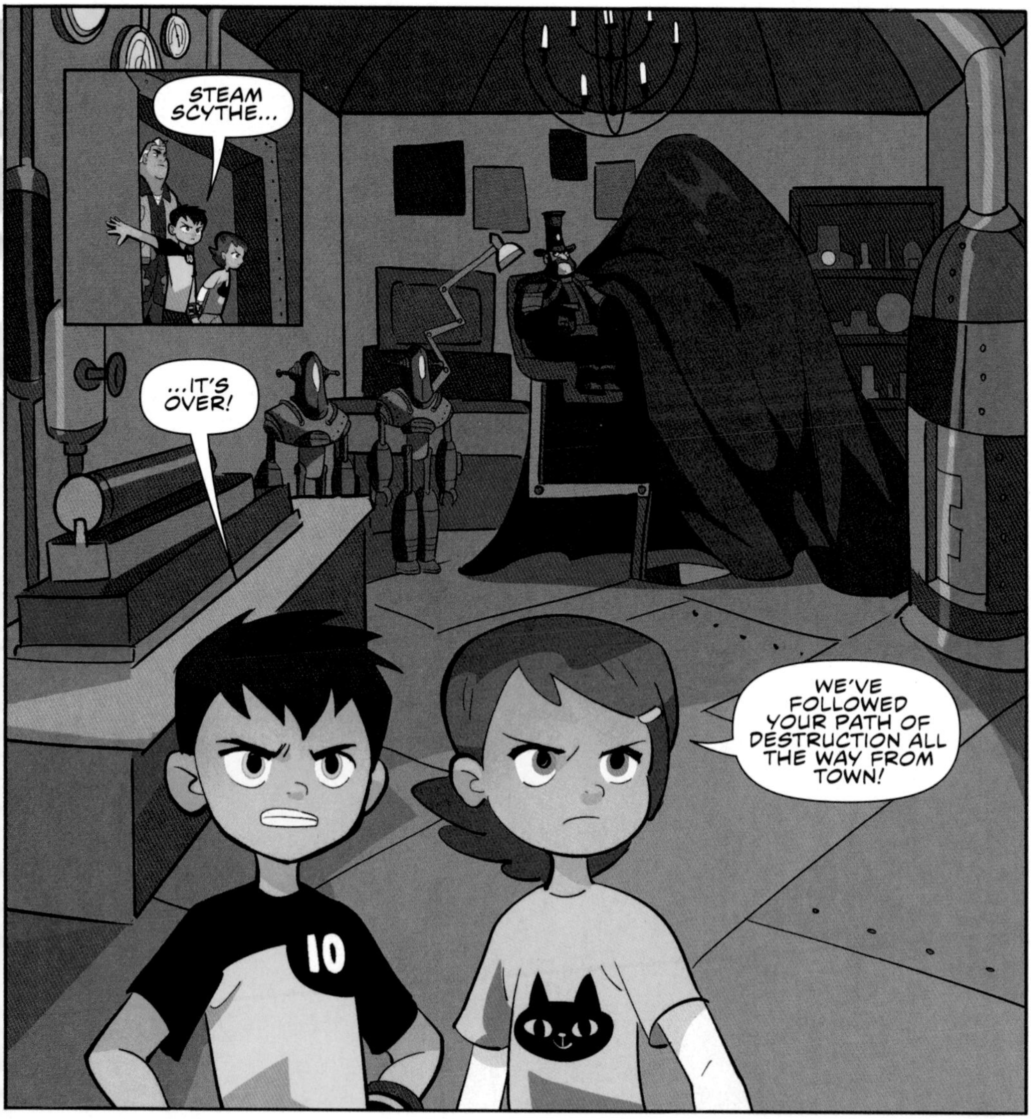
STEAM SCYTHE...
...IT'S OVER!
WE'VE FOLLOWED YOUR PATH OF DESTRUCTION ALL THE WAY FROM TOWN!
10
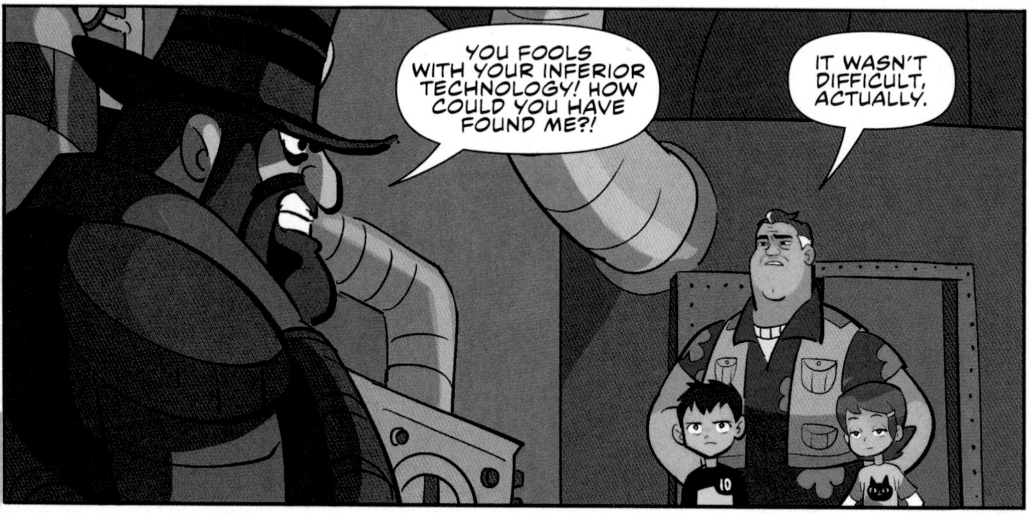
YOU FOOLS WITH YOUR INFERIOR TECHNOLOGY! HOW COULD YOU HAVE FOUND ME?!
IT WASN'T DIFFICULT, ACTUALLY.
10

"YOU WEREN'T VERY SUBTLE."

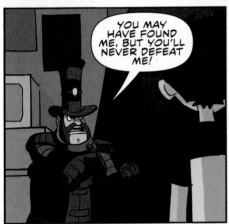

YOU MAY HAVE FOUND ME, BUT YOU'LL NEVER DEFEAT ME!

WE'LL SEE ABOUT THAT!

MECHANOIDS!! ATTACK!

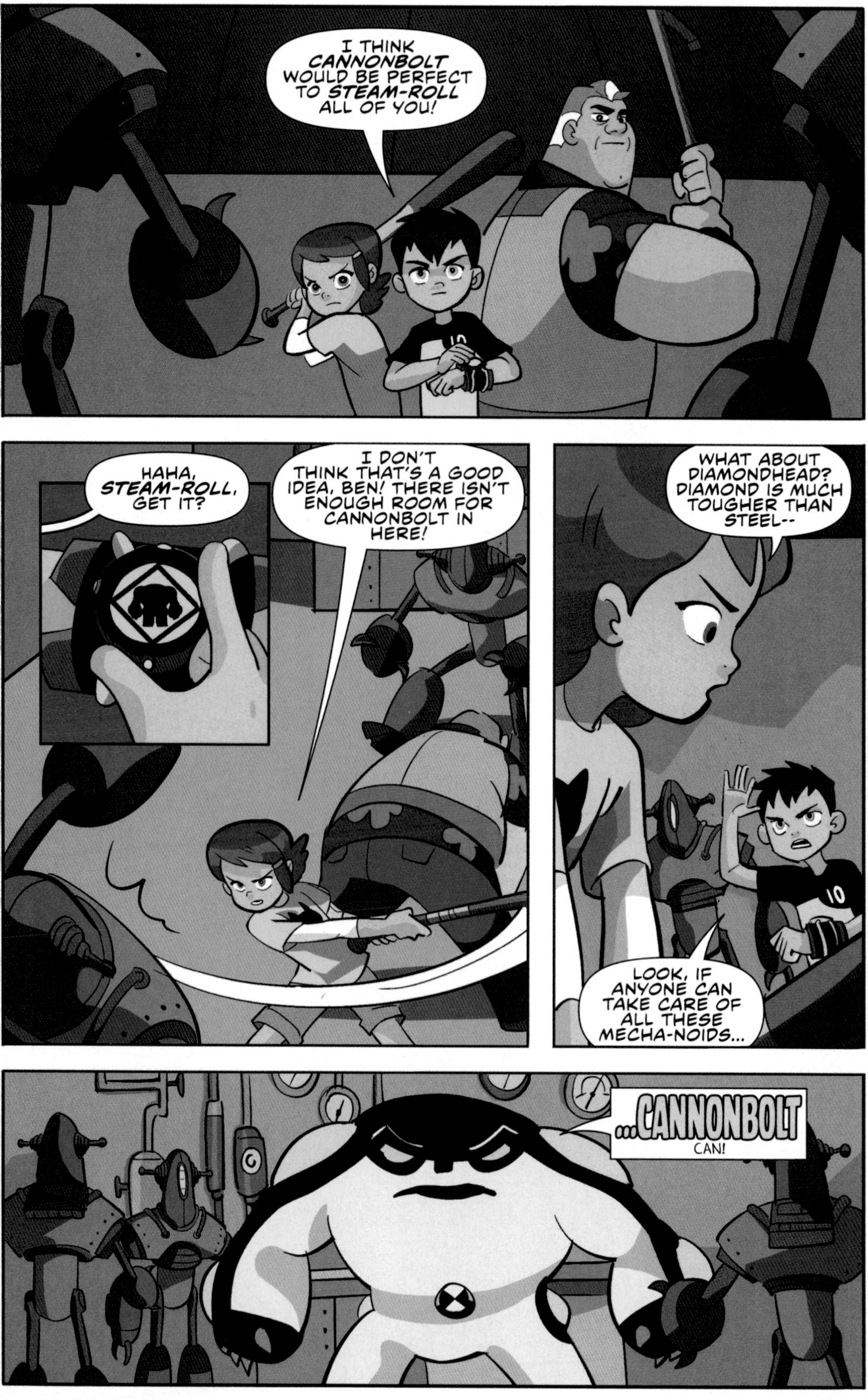
I THINK CANNONBOLT WOULD BE PERFECT TO STEAM-ROLL ALL OF YOU!
HAHA, STEAM-ROLL, GET IT?
I DON'T THINK THAT'S A GOOD IDEA, BEN! THERE ISN'T ENOUGH ROOM FOR CANNONBOLT IN HERE!
WHAT ABOUT DIAMONDHEAD? DIAMOND IS MUCH TOUGHER THAN STEEL--
LOOK, IF ANYONE CAN TAKE CARE OF ALL THESE MECHA-NOIDS...
...CANNONBOLT CAN!

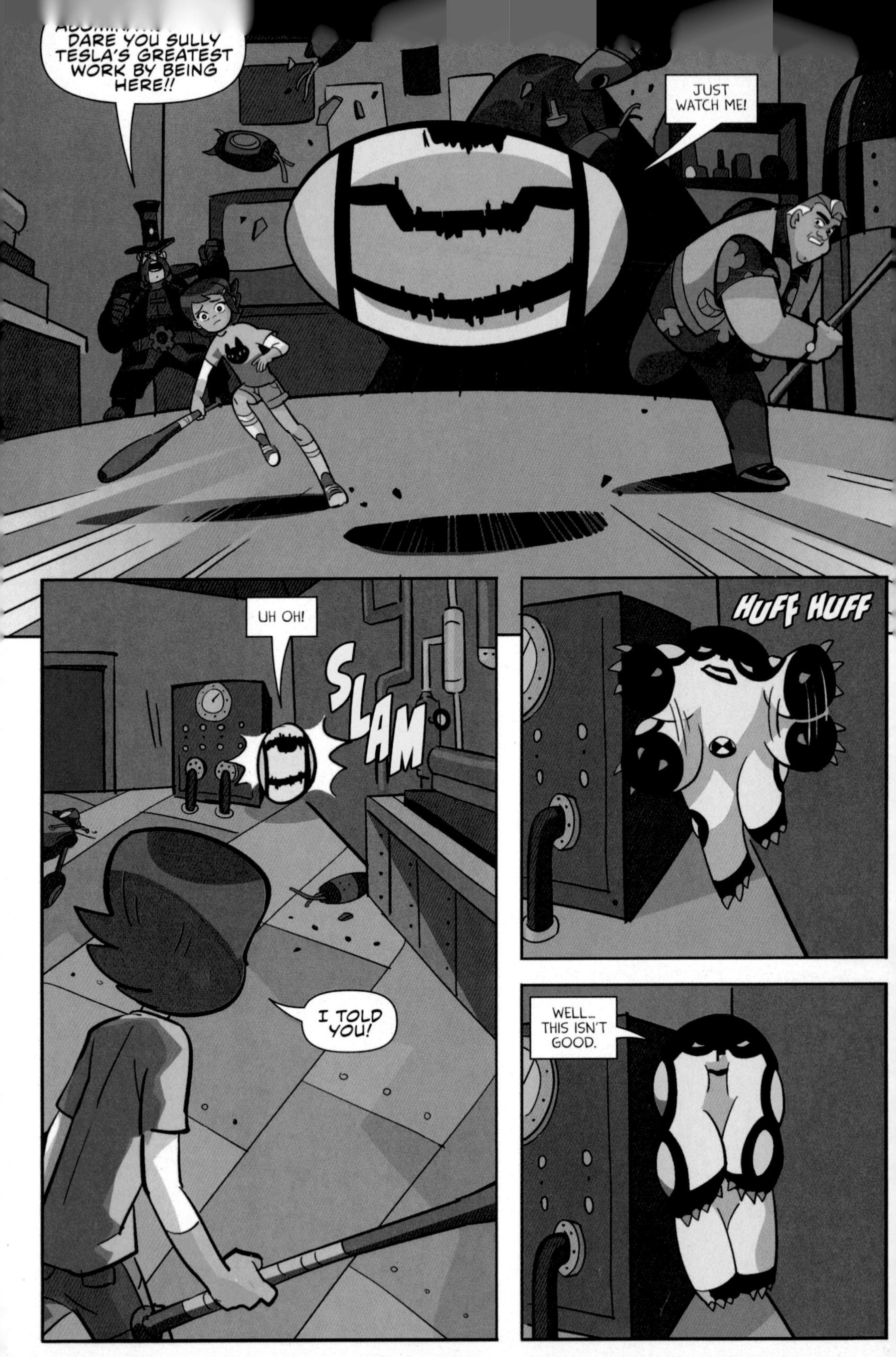
DARE YOU SULLY TESLA'S GREATEST WORK BY BEING HERE!!
JUST WATCH ME!
UH OH!
SLAM
I TOLD YOU!
HUFF HUFF
WELL... THIS ISN'T GOOD.

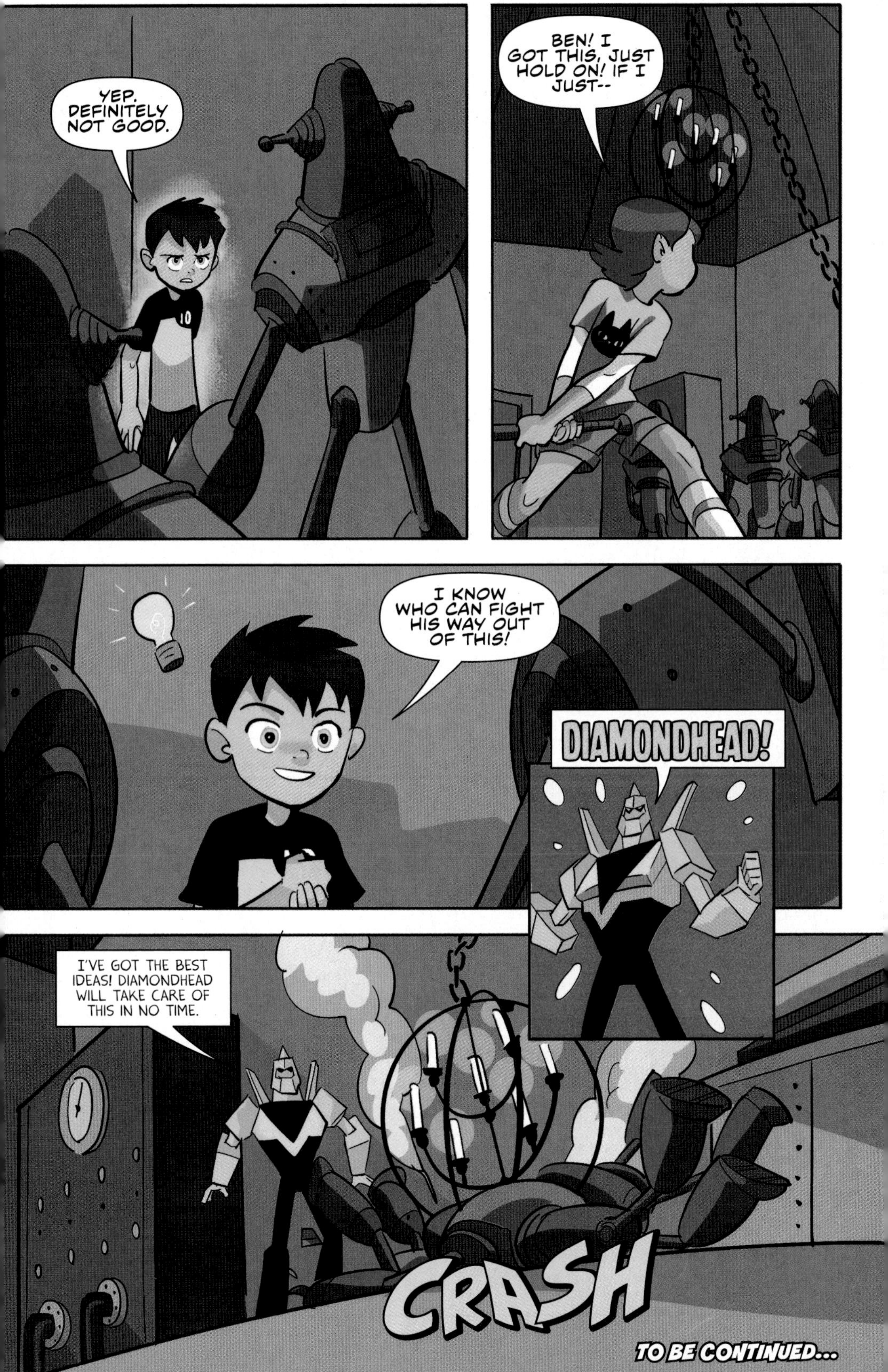
YEP. DEFINITELY NOT GOOD.
BEN! I GOT THIS, JUST HOLD ON! IF I JUST--
I KNOW WHO CAN FIGHT HIS WAY OUT OF THIS!
DIAMONDHEAD!
I'VE GOT THE BEST IDEAS! DIAMONDHEAD WILL TAKE CARE OF THIS IN NO TIME.
CRASH
TO BE CONTINUED...

DISCOVER
EXPLOSIVE NEW WORLDS

Adventure Time
Pendleton Ward and Others
Volume 1
ISBN: 978-1-60886-280-1 | $14.99 US
Volume 2
ISBN: 978-1-60886-323-5 | $14.99 US
Adventure Time: Islands
ISBN: 978-1-60886-972-5 | $9.99 US

The Amazing World of Gumball
Ben Bocquelet and Others
Volume 1
ISBN: 978-1-60886-488-1 | $14.99 US
Volume 2
ISBN: 978-1-60886-793-6 | $14.99 US

Brave Chef Brianna
Sam Sykes, Selina Espiritu
ISBN: 978-1-68415-050-2 | $14.99 US

Mega Princess
Kelly Thompson, Brianne Drouhard
ISBN: 978-1-68415-007-6 | $14.99 US

The Not-So Secret Society
*Matthew Daley, Arlene Daley,
Wook Jin Clark*
ISBN: 978-1-60886-997-8 | $9.99 US

Over the Garden Wall
*Patrick McHale, Jim Campbell
and Others*
Volume 1
ISBN: 978-1-60886-940-4 | $14.99 US
Volume 2
ISBN: 978-1-68415-006-9 | $14.99 US

Steven Universe
Rebecca Sugar and Others
Volume 1
ISBN: 978-1-60886-706-6 | $14.99 US
Volume 2
ISBN: 978-1-60886-796-7 | $14.99 US

Steven Universe & The Crystal Gems
ISBN: 978-1-60886-921-3 | $14.99 US

Steven Universe: Too Cool for School
ISBN: 978-1-60886-771-4 | $14.99 US

**AVAILABLE AT YOUR LOCAL
COMICS SHOP AND BOOKSTORE**
To find a comics shop in your area, visit www.comicshoplocator.com
WWW.BOOM-STUDIOS.COM